CW00409752

FIRST TO BID

UNRAVELED, BOOK 2

MARIE JOHNSTON

LE PUBLISHING

First to Bid

Copyright 2018 as Highest Bidder by Marie Johnston

Editing by Razor Sharp Editing

Cover Art by Secret Identity Graphics

2nd Edition proofing by My Brother's Editor and Double Author Services

The characters, places, and events in this story are fictional. Any similarities to real people, places, or events are coincidental and unintentional.

❀ Created with Vellum

CHAPTER 1

lynn

I WHISTLED as I maneuvered my extended-cab Chevy pickup into a parking spot at the edge of the lot. I killed the engine and jumped out. My gaze snagged on my black wingtips and the yellow lines on the pavement a few feet away. I might have taken up three, maybe four, parking spots with my crooked parking job. I briefly considered getting back in and rearranging it, but less chance at door dings this way, and I was parked at the end. Fewer chances of making it difficult for other drivers to maneuver around me and this lot was only full around Christmas and during special promotional events. It'd be fine, but people might assume I'm a dick for the park job.

With a shrug, I strode toward the comic book store.

If I wanted to hang out with my best friend Wes, I had to kick it with the fanboys who flocked to Arcadia. Wes's wife, Mara owned the comic book and gaming shop, and Arcadia had become a second home to me. But browsing through the latest releases wasn't what I was here for today. Mara was sponsoring the first annual Bachelors for Dollars fundraiser, and I had been the first recruit.

I reached the glass door and held it open for an attractive woman breezing out. She was in the middle of putting on her sunglasses and paused when she caught sight of me. I flashed her a grin. She flushed and rushed out with a quick "thanks."

I eyed the sashay of her hips in the gauzy dress she wore. *Dayum*. If that was the type of woman who would be bidding on me, well...maybe Wes wouldn't owe me as much as I had let on. Next year they might have bachelorettes. Then I'd have to sit out and do some bidding—for charity's sake, of course.

Inside the store, my eyes didn't need any time to adjust. The floor-to-ceiling windows of the store kept the space bright and airy, giving it the illusion of way more square footage than it had. But the size was still admirable, enough to organize comic books, host gaming days, and even hold small conventions. I should know. I'd built it, had been involved in its construction since its inception.

Scanning the place, I spotted Mara in the corner chatting with a woman a few inches taller than her with sandy-brown hair in double ponytails and jean shorts hitched up by suspenders. A gaudy tote hung off her shoulder.

The woman had a nice ass. My gaze lingered a moment before the giant *W*s on her tote grabbed my attention. A Wonder Woman fan. I could respect her taste. Aside from her atrocious style, I envied her clothing. The mercury crawled higher each day as we headed into summer, and while my suit was the best money could buy, a suit jacket was never my first choice once the snow melted.

But clients expected this level of professionalism before entrusting me with millions of dollars. Because they sure didn't expect me to be the one swinging the hammer, so the jackets, ties, and uncomfortable shoes were there to stay. Only four more days until the weekend—and clothes I wouldn't sweat in. I needed it to be Friday already.

"Hey, Flynn." Chris, the co-owner of the store, stocked a wall of dice in all different shapes and colors. Just like I dress to impress future clients, Chris dressed for his job—a Batman shirt and worn blue jeans. His hair was a half-inch short of being shaggy and he looked like he was barely thirty, but Mara said he has a kid who's a teenager.

"Chris, how's the building holding up?" I asked him the same thing every time. Every structure I build had an unspoken warranty. Any work attributed to me and my firm got my full backing.

"Great. That little leak you repaired in the sunroof last week never stood a chance."

"Thanks for telling me."

Chris gave me a knowing nod. Mara would've hired someone to take care of the problem. She thought she was taking advantage of me. She was wrong. Getting my hands dirty was like a special treat.

I found Wes restocking the newest *Doctor Strange* comics. "What the hell, dude? Doesn't Mara hire people to do that?" No one would know that a guy worth a cool billion was sorting their comics.

Wes arched a dark brow. "Mara asked me to pull your order, fucker. I figured it'd be just as easy to put the whole box out while I was at it. Besides, she's busy with the lady she's organizing the fundraiser with, so it's either this or stand around looking like a creeper."

I snickered. Wes couldn't creep if he tried. He was more likely to get asked for an autograph again by little kids who thought he was Clark Kent. No glasses, but Wes's slicked black hair and piercing blue eyes were straight out of the DC universe.

I sorted through the pile of comics. "So, did you get my pulls? Doctor Strange and Justice League?"

Wes slapped my hand away. "Yes. Perks of being friends with the boss. Your stack is in the back and I already charged your card."

Sweet. At least I'd have some reading material until a generous lady bought me for the week. Hitting the clubs wasn't the same without my wingman. Without Wes to BS with until I caught a sexy woman's eye, sitting around Wes's club, Canon—or, hell, any club—smacked of lonely desperation. But it edged out sitting at home and listening to not a damn thing.

The downfall of having built my own house—there wasn't anything to do but watch HGTV. No projects, nothing to maintain. I'd built a top-of-the-line, luxurious home. Working with my hands and building shit was all I knew how to do. I'd even trolled a few rummage sales and thrift stores, looking for furniture to flip.

Then what? Have the most junkyard-chic house to show all of no one?

Nah. I'd rather get laid instead of sitting at home, watching my superhero movie marathons. Which were happening more and more often lately... Last weekend, I'd even abandoned my efforts to find a willing partner and gone home for a Thor marathon.

I'd had a headache. That was it. It'd been low-grade, hadn't even needed a Tylenol, but, well, I was the boss. I didn't get sick days. If I didn't bring money in, no one else would get paid.

The woman talking to Mara guffawed, her head thrown back, ponytails swinging, the sound infectious. A joyous laugh that almost made me smile for no reason.

I jutted my chin toward the women. "Is it okay to interrupt? Mara wanted my picture with some merchandise for the auction flyer."

"They're waiting for you. Tilly wanted to be here when we took the photos. It means a lot to her that people are willing to do the auction."

"That's the abused adult center lady?"

Wes gave me a droll look. "Tilly Johnson is a *teacher*, but yes, she and Mara are raising funds for the abused adult resource center. For the kids there, more specifically. The money will go towards clothing and school supplies, even basic medical care."

I shoved my hands in the pockets of my slacks and adjusted my shoulders to loosen the tightness in my chest. A woman who gave a shit about kids. Of course, people cared about kids, but I couldn't help but admire those who went out of their way to help them.

I mentally shook down the rise of unwanted memories. This Tilly Johnson was a better person than me, but that didn't mean I had to let the same old feelings haunt me. I had the best of both worlds—helping an organization that helped disadvantaged kids but without people wondering why I was doing it. I usually stuck to sponsorships of sports teams so I could plaster my company's name, Halstengard Industries, everywhere. I would straight-up donate, but with the amounts I gave, charities sometimes tracked me down, and the last thing I wanted to do was explain why I supported their cause—or worse, have people investigate my personal life. But this was a bachelor auction. I was rich and single. There was no need to explain why I was helping.

"Come on. Mara set up a little corner for the photos." Wes tucked the empty box under his arm, looking completely out of place in a suit like the one I was wearing, only Wes had taken his jacket and tie off. I couldn't wait to shed my navy blue pinstriped suit. I hadn't so much as loosened my tie yet.

I followed him to a bench surrounded by action figures and posters, the backdrop for a photo that would be handed out to prospective bidders on Friday night. "Why didn't we do this earlier? Might've been good for promo."

"Yeah. They put this thing together pretty quickly. Tilly works through the summer but had a little time between school letting out and...whatever work she's doing for the next couple of months. We figured we'd give it a shot and if it's successful, we can organize and promote a bigger event for next year. We only recruited five people to auction off. Best to keep it small in case it's an epic fail."

Instead of perching on the bench, I set one foot on it and leaned on my knee. Wes smirked but picked up the camera.

"Between you and me," I said, "I got a cabin with two bedrooms just in case my highest bidder is...you know."

Wes sighed, then chuckled. "Is that your new form of safe sex?"

I shrugged. "We'll see. Who knows? Sometimes any sex is better than no sex, but I wanted an out just in case."

"So sure the woman will be ready to jump you?"

"You don't drop a few grand on this," I swept my hands down the body I shaped with brutal workout sessions, "and not want some. But seriously, it's a bachelor auction. I'd be naïve not to plan for either scenario."

"No matter how it turns out, I appreciate you supporting Mara like this."

I lifted my chin in a bro-nod. Better than getting choked up with emotion.

The auction fit my carefree persona and maybe I'd end up with a hot chick dying to spend a fun week at the lake with me. Then we could part ways with the built-in excuse that hey, the deal was just for a vacay. I'd never want a woman willing to buy me for charity to feel pressured into putting out.

"Flynn Halstengard?" a shrill female voice rang out. "Oh. My. God. It's really you!"

I froze. The woman Mara had been talking to was charging toward me. My eyes went wide. *Fuuuuck.* I know her.

"Tulip?" I squeaked.

A look of alarm passed over her expression before her smile returned. "Um, no. It's just Tilly now."

Tilly Johnson was Crazy J from high school? How— What— Now her clothing made sense. Tulip had never had any fashion sense. The knee-high white socks, athletic shoes, and too-short jean shorts fit Tulip Johnson perfectly.

She'd moved away our senior year, and only then had I found peace after the three long years she'd dogged my footsteps, pining for me in her bat-shit crazy way.

I must've been gaping like a beached walleye because Mara's gaze darted from me to Wes, finally settling on Wes to beg him to think of something. I couldn't speak. I'd been teased mercilessly over the antics Tulip had pulled trying to get my attention in high school. And those were just her actions toward *me.* She'd done enough cringe-worthy things to wreak havoc with her reputation. Her one-woman sit-in at the local animal pound that euthanized unclaimed cats and dogs had gotten her mercilessly teased. That was the incident that had seemed to garner the worst attention. The reigning mean girl had been throwing kitty litter at a sobbing Tulip in the girls' locker room. Crazy J's cries could be heard from the boys' locker room. I'd barged in, seen what was happening, and dumped the bag on the queen bee's head. Crazy J had crushed on me hard after that.

Before graduation, I'd landed in the mean girl's bed for a round or two. What was her name? As forgettable as the sex, apparently. But I'd never forgotten Crazy J—unfortunately. And here she was.

Tulip—*Tilly*—gasped as her wide, steel-blue eyes took me and my surroundings in, then the camera Wes held as his traitorous friend stood with a perplexed and morbidly curious expression. She clapped her hands. "Are you one of the bachelors? *Seriously?*"

"Y-yes," I stammered. *Get it together, dude.* This girl still left me floundering.

She shrieked a giggle and he winced. Yep, same laugh. "Looks like I know who I'm bidding on."

My face went cold as all the blood drained from it. No. Just *no*. I couldn't spend an entire week with Crazy J.

~

Tilly

I COULD SO SPEND a week with Flynn!

Gawd. He looked better than ever like he'd just stepped out of a catalog. His face had matured from hot teen to muscular man in full possession of his smolder.

Now I knew what had possessed me that day a year ago when I'd come to Arcadia looking for some classroom items. The kids I taught didn't learn traditionally, and graphic novels were easier and more interesting to read than standard kids' books. Mara and I had struck up a friendship and I had kept coming back. My students loved the items I brought back to class, and I loved being able to claim a friend, albeit one kept at arm's length.

Then I'd rattled on about my idea for a bachelor auction and Mara and her uber-sexy husband had rounded up willing participants.

It was fate. I had savings to donate but hadn't thought of bidding—but to finally get a date with Flynn Halstengard? Heck, yeah!

My knight with platinum hair as bright as shining armor was finally attainable.

Wow. I couldn't quit ogling him, but then I'd never thought we'd cross paths again. My line of failed relationships wasn't his fault, of course, but I couldn't help but wonder how the lame sex with them would compare to sex with Flynn. He had to be dynamite in bed and I could use some sparks between the sheets that didn't include my vibrator shorting out.

My cheeks were starting to hurt from grinning. Flynn stared at me like he was dumbfounded. I had no idea why— *Oh*.

Of all the days. It was Wacky Monday at school and I'd done it up good. I kept a pack of men's socks just for these days and my mom-jeans-turned-shorts were pulled up so high my nethers were numb. All sorts of buttons I'd collected over the years were pinned to my suspenders, but at least I'd left my tiara in my car. It was one of thirty. Because a girl could never have too many tiaras.

"I'm totally going to bid on you," I burst out. How awesome. I could donate *and* have a chance with Flynn, too! One week with him would see me through another long summer until school started again.

"Y-you don't have to." Flynn's stammer was just as adorable as I remembered.

I could've done without him calling me Tulip, though. He hadn't stuttered over that. That name brought back too many memories. I even hated the flower.

His gaze swept down to my scuffed shoes and I wanted to groan, to tell him that I didn't normally dress like this, but that would be a lie. My students responded well to my outfits so I kept up my zany appearance. Lord knew, there was no other reason in my life to dress up. Except for this Friday night. My grin broadened.

My phone *pinged* inside of the large Wonder Woman tote draped over my shoulder. "Oh!"

Flynn jumped, and I wanted to sigh. Why was he always so nervous around me? He had smooth-talked teachers and other students. His pals had followed his lead—he had been the jock at the head of the pack. As an adult, he probably *killed* it. Yet with me, he withdrew into a nervous shell.

But then, I kinda had that effect on other adults. Mara seemed genuinely entertained, and Wes was the only guy who talked to me like I was another human being and not an alien from the planet Moron. Even my students' parents could be patronizing or dismissive. But still better than what I'd grown up with, so I couldn't complain. No, I *wouldn't* complain. I'd been given a new lease on life and I wasn't going to squander it.

Digging my phone out, I checked the time. Yep, my alarm had gone off.

"I have a tutoring session." I turned to Mara for a quick hug. "Thank you so much for making this happen." Then I met Flynn's green gaze, my kryptonite. "And I'll see *you* on Friday night."

He didn't smile, but his eyes got wider. Wasn't he relieved to at least know who was going to win him? Because I was *so* going to win him! Better me than a stranger, right?

As I walked out of the store, I pondered his reaction. He'd be okay spending the week with me, wouldn't he? It's not like I wanted him to profess his undying love, sweep me off my feet, and make love to me for my happily ever after.

I hadn't dreamed that at all for the last…decade…and a half. Not at all.

Tearing my hair out of its ponytails, I slid into the driver's seat of my car. I shook my hair out and twisted it into a bun. With an eye on the time, I dug bobby pins out of my cup holder and stabbed them into my hair. Next, the suspenders came off and I dug through my tote for a lacy cardigan to go over my T-shirt. After I shrugged that on, I toed off my shoes and rolled off my socks. I sighed in relief as cool air blew across my legs. I put on the sandals I produced from my tote and fired up the engine.

As I drove out of the lot, I frowned at the big truck taking up so many spaces. Someone was likely compensating for some deficiency in his ego.

Not my problem. I drove as fast as legally possible to a large, sprawling house in a prestigious gated community. My stomach clenched the closer I got.

The kid under that roof taxed all of my special-needs skills. But the little boy's parents were a whole different challenge. I had shown up once in my standard wacky wear and the woman's haughty stare had withered me in my knee-high socks. Then the dad… The sky was the limit for my anxiety whenever he was around. The more sedate and boring I dressed, the more Mr. Woods hit on me—often in front of his wife.

If I didn't know any better, I'd just assume rich people sucked, but as my past proved, bad behavior wasn't confined to any particular income bracket.

I parked in the large circular drive, jumped out, and trotted to the door.

I took a moment to compose my breathing and pat stray hairs down before I rang the bell. The door swung open.

"Miss Tilly," greeted the housekeeper, Berta.

"I'm not late!" I smiled and rushed past her toward Charlie's muffled cries.

"It won't matter," Berta murmured.

The first time Berta had made such a bold comment, I

had almost dropped in surprise. But unlike me, who stuck around for Charlie, Berta could move on and find a new job. A trustworthy housekeeper was in high demand. It was harder for me to find clients who'd pay me the wage I requested and for long-term work.

"Miss Tilly. You're finally here." Mrs. Woods's nasal voice rang off the walls.

I squared my shoulders as Mrs. Woods's heels clacked against the marble floor into the entryway. I half expected "The Imperial March" to play in the background, but Charlie's wails would've drowned it out.

The woman's snide gaze evaluated me and, from the crease in her brow, found me lacking. Like usual. Charlie's cries hit a crescendo, then died down. I twitched to run to him but had to finish with my employer.

Mrs. Woods pushed her auburn hair off her face and I blinked. Had the woman's hand been shaking?

"He's in fine form today." Mrs. Woods bypassed me and started up the stairs. "You'd better get in there before he hurts himself."

I jogged to the special room Charlie's parents had set up for him. Inside, the five-year-old was rocking in the corner, self-soothing. His wails had subsided. I rushed to his side but didn't touch him. He wasn't always open to physical comfort. He drew in on himself and turned away. After several minutes, I coaxed him out. From the blank look in his eyes, I shouldn't be too ambitious in my teachings today.

Okay, so calm playtime instead. I could make it educational.

Charlie snatched up an alphabet block and I frowned. A red welt was swelling at his temple. It'd be black and blue in a few hours. Dang. Had he hurt himself before I'd gotten in here? He wouldn't tolerate ice, so I continued with what tutoring I could.

Once my hour was up, I stepped out and called for Berta.

When the woman came into view, I pointed up the stairs. "Think I can talk to her?"

Berta scoffed. "Are you kidding? Charlie's evening nanny arrives in ten minutes. Mrs. Woods is out for the count."

My shoulders slumped. "Can you tell her that Charlie must've banged his head during his fit?"

"Of course, of course." Berta dropped her voice. "Go on home. She doesn't pay you for her deadbeat-mom hours."

I coughed back a chuckle. "I can hang around for ten minutes. It's no problem." Charlie might seem like he was in his own world most of the time, but he didn't need to be alone constantly. I doubted the nanny did more than sit and do her homework and ward off Mr. Woods's advances—or not. I played with Charlie for fifteen more minutes before his nanny arrived and I updated her.

Back out in the late-spring air, I inhaled a long, deep breath. For the first time, I felt optimistic. I'd meticulously plotted and saved to pay back every cent that the center had sunk into my failure of a childhood. Now I could hand it over and get a date with Flynn in the process.

A smile spread across my face. Things were finally starting to look up.

lynn

I STRAIGHTENED the bow tie of my tux. My stomach somersaulted and I bounced in my wingtips. Each minute that went by in the small back room of Arcadia felt like an hour. In a few minutes, I'd have to go out and strut down the runway while women fought over me. Please, let my plan work. I could not spend eight days with Crazy J.

My phone rang and I jerked it from my pocket. My nerves were going to kill me. "Halstengard."

My biggest client greeted me on the other end. "I know it's the weekend, but I'd like to touch base with you on the bank project."

"Of course," I said because whatever John Woods wanted, John Woods got. "How's—"

Before I could rattle off a time, a shriek on the other end of the phone pierced my eardrum.

John swore. "Guess it'll have to wait until Monday. The nanny has the night off and my kid's melting down."

"Not a problem, sir." I wasn't ashamed to kiss ass when my company name and fifty million were on the line. "Just give me a couple of hours' notice. I'll be at my lake cabin all next week, but it's close enough to the cities I can meet you." I'd made sure I had good cell reception at my vacation home just so I could be accessible to clients.

"Yeah, okay, maybe I'll call tomorrow." The wails grew stronger. "Ah, shit. Monday at eleven, at your office."

"Monday at eleven." I hung up and tucked my phone away. At least my date would get a vacation if I couldn't, which was why I'd chosen a lake getaway instead of the Caribbean. I was never far from work, and I tried not to quit working, just like I avoided being home alone with nothing to do. Idle time only let my mind think about the past, and the present I couldn't forget.

A knock on the door jolted me out of my reverie. I opened it to a pretty brunette with a dress laminated over her banging bod. My backup plan.

"Becky, thank God."

Her brows knit together and she tilted her head. "Flynn."

"Okay, it's just like my text said, all you have to do is outbid everyone. I'll cover the cost. I've already arranged it with the owner."

Wes had oozed disappointment and shaken his head, but something about my insistence had registered. *"I'm not hiding this from Mara, but I'll kill you if Tilly finds out you duped her."*

I could live with that.

My soon-to-be vacation buddy narrowed her eyes on me. "Mm-kay."

I flashed my most dazzling grin. "I'll make it worth your while, Becky." She knew how well we worked together in bed, it was why I'd chosen her for my desperate SOS.

Whether she slept with me again, I didn't care. She'd get a vacation and Tilly wouldn't waste her money on a guy who wasn't interested in her—and she'd never know.

Instead of a smile in return, Becky scrutinized me for a moment before sauntering away.

I swallowed a moment of guilt. Of course, I didn't want to hurt Crazy J's feelings. She always seemed to have the best intentions, but then she blatantly stomped all over the limits. I couldn't let her win out of pity, couldn't delude myself that she'd be able to walk away after spending one-on-one time together, not after the way she crushed on me in high school and the way she reacted after seeing me again. This was best for her.

Then why did I feel like what I was doing was insulting and seedy?

It was a little underhanded, and I owned it. I always owned my work. The plan had been laid out for Becky in my message before I'd agreed. She knew what she was getting into, but I had to admit I was afraid Tulip—*Tilly* would find out. If she did, then dammit, I'd explain it. I didn't run from the hard times. Not anymore. I had built my business from the motherfucking bottom with a nail gun, and I'd done it all honestly.

Wes popped into the doorway. "Ready, bachelor number five?"

I straightened my tie for the twentieth time. I wished I could've roamed the floor and worked the crowd, but Mara had felt that might start too much drama. She'd passed the flyers around with our stats and the details of our getaways. Now for my debut.

I followed Wes to the showroom. Blinking into the dim crowd of people, the nervous flutter that preceded my almost-cured stuttering problem flared. Hopefully, I wouldn't have to speak.

Wes took a stance in front of the microphone and I posed next to him. I scanned the audience but couldn't find Crazy J. I mentally reprimanded myself. Probably should try to call her Tilly. Didn't feel right. Tulip fits her much better. A bright flower that bloomed despite the dullness around it.

God, was I going to start spouting poetry?

I kept searching and finally found Becky, her spectacular cleavage on display. I shot her a smile, but she just narrowed her eyes at me and looked around. Was she searching for the crazy lady I'd described?

"And now we have bachelor number five." Wes's deep voice quieted the murmurs in the crowd. Then someone let out a wolf whistle.

My gaze was drawn to the catcaller. Opposite the platform from Becky stood a pretty young woman in a flowery, flowing dress that stood out among the typical cocktail dresses.

Wes's introduction droned on as I squinted at her. The woman might not be dressed as fancy, but she held herself well. The elegant twist in her light brown hair bared a slender neck, and as much as I wanted to let my gaze drift down her body to what must be spectacular legs, I had to see her face. When she caught my gaze and smiled wide, my heart seized.

Holy. Shit.

Tulip "Crazy J" Johnson. And I'd just checked her out.

I ripped my gaze away and aimed my smile at someone else. Anyone else. Any female from twenty to eighty, I didn't care. I needed to be on my game and Tilly messed with my mind.

"Now with all that out of the way, who's going to open the bid at five hundred?" Wes said, both of us looking out at the crowd.

Several paddles rose. But Becky hadn't moved.

"Do I have one thousand?"

Fewer paddles now. Still not Becky, but she was probably holding out until she had to step in.

Wes played up the crowd and the tension almost stopped my pulse. "Nice, ladies. The Center for Abuse Recovery and Arcadia thanks you all for your generosity. With that being said, who wants a lazy lake vacation for two thousand dollars?"

Three paddles waved. One was a lady as old as my grandma. Another was a cute lady in a tight dress—totally my type. The third was Tulip.

I glanced at Becky. She stood with her arms folded and a brow arched.

I swallowed.

"Two thousand five hundred?" Wes asked.

"Ten thousand, two hundred and twenty-eight dollars," Tulip called out. "And fifty-five cents."

My brows popped up. Murmurs of approval passed through the crowd. My first thought was that the odd number was a typical Tulip bid. My next thought was to wave frantically at Becky. Could she hear me yelling "Bid twenty thousand!" in my head?

Wes shot me a rueful look. "Do we have ten thousand, two hundred twenty-eight dollars, and fifty-six cents?"

No paddles went up. Tulip craned her head around, her brow creased with worry.

I caught Becky's gaze and arched my brow.

She stood on her tiptoes to lean on the stage, her expression was partly pissed, partly smug. "Becky's my sister, asshole."

A cold bucket of panic dropped over me. I'd called her the wrong name? Oh, *shit*. Becky was blond, and she had a sister —Samantha—who I'd slept with a couple of years before I'd hooked up with Becky. I learned later that they were related. Had I mixed up their contact info? Aw, hell, I'd fucked up.

"*Sorry*," I mouthed, but it was a piss poor apology. How the hell do I apologize for something like that? It was a dick move. This plan wasn't supposed to end with someone getting their feelings hurt.

She gave me a *fuck off* look and spun around, marching through the crowd, leaving my ass behind.

Frantically, I used my eyes to plead with the crowd. I wiggled my tie and forced a tense smile. "Come on, ladies. It's for a good cause." I couldn't stand a week of hero-worship in Tulip's eyes. Not toward me. I was the last person to deserve it.

"Going once…" Wes called.

"Ladies, ladies. I'm the only bachelor with more than a weekend getaway." I swallowed hard. I'd gotten Samantha's hopes up and hurt her. She'd counted on me. Dammit, this was why I didn't date or do relationships. I messed them all up.

Now Tulip was giving me a look I definitely didn't deserve, one full of trust and excitement that cut into dark places I couldn't revisit.

A week, strings-free. That was all I wanted. That was all I could give.

"Going twice…" Wes waited two more seconds before holding his arm out to Tulip. Her eyes were bright and her smile ecstatic. She jumped up and down.

"To the highest bidder goes Flynn Halstengard. Congratulations, Tilly Johnson."

Tilly

. . .

19

OMGGGGG!!

I squealed and threw my hands up in the air. Flynn's mouth hung open. Was he in awe of the amount I'd spent on him?

This was going to be the biggest check I'd ever written and so dang worth it!

Me. And Flynn. For a week!

I'd barely glanced at the flyers for the other bachelors that had made their rounds through all the bidders. But Flynn's prize package was a week at Lake Webber. It was halfway between Minneapolis and Itasca State Park. I'd never been there, but then I'd never been outside of the Twin Cities and their surrounding suburbs.

Would he teach me how to fish? Ooh, I'd always wanted to go hiking. And boating. Fishing on a boat!

This was the most excited I'd been in my adult life—in my whole life.

Flynn disappeared backstage as Wes wrapped up the auction portion of the night. I worked through the throng of people to find Mara.

Mara was at the counter, accepting checks from the highest bidders. Her cocktail dress had a Batman emblem sewn on the front. I looked down at my thrift-store dress. I hadn't expected the auction to be as fancy as the black tuxes the bachelors wore and the formal wear of the attendees. But it's not like I wasn't used to standing out in a crowd.

If only I had the money to bling-out cool clothing like Mara. At my friend's encouragement, I'd ordered a few pairs of superhero leggings. The kids got a kick out of them, but they weren't who I wanted to impress tonight—and I'd known enough not to wear them under my dress.

Mara smiled as I approached. The poor woman must be tired. Mara had taken my idea and done the majority of the work. Her pleasant expression seemed tight, but it must just be fatigue.

"So…you bought Flynn, huh?" Mara asked.

Tilly smiled so wide it could've cracked her face in half. "Yes. I can't wait."

"About Flynn." Mara hesitated and glanced at the now-empty stage. "When I met Wes, he wasn't in a good place in his life. He was angry, self-absorbed, and…frankly, he was an asshole. We had a rough start. Well, we had an awesome start, but our rough patch was a shitstorm." She pursed her lips like she wasn't sure how to say her next words. "I get that feeling about Flynn, that he isn't ready for…a thing with someone else, that life is too much about himself."

Flynn, an asshole? Had he changed so much over the years? No, a kid who had raced into the girls' locker room and saved me from littergeddon couldn't have changed that much.

I flashed my most reassuring smile. "I'm sure he'll be a gentleman all week. I have faith in Flynn."

Mara snorted. "Flynn, a gentleman?" She leveled me with a serious stare. "I've seen how Flynn can be with women, and I don't want to see you get hurt."

A flash of irritation zinged through me. Why did people always assume I was an innocent noob? I had experienced the dark side of people, had been betrayed by those who were supposed to love and protect me. Sorry-not-sorry, Flynn could never be as bad as my parents had been.

I dug my already completed check from my purse. "Maybe I'll be the one breaking his heart."

Mara looked like she was about to argue, but I didn't care to hear it. I set the check down and flounced away.

I had thought Mara was a friend who'd treat me like an equal, but at the first chance, she'd used kid gloves, thinking I didn't know better.

Yes, I was ecstatic to have a date with Flynn. For an entire week! But I was just as excited about the week of vacation. Summers were always difficult, with the absence of my teaching wages. I'd always filled my time with a couple of part-time jobs, places that were willing to hire me for only a few months, or to fill in during holiday breaks. I'd worked my ass off building a clientele for my tutoring business, and for the last couple of years, I'd been able to get by with just my tutoring income and even keep a few weekends to myself. But never had I been brave enough to take an entire week of no pay.

Many attendees were filing out. A few of the winners chatted up their bachelors. I scanned those remaining but couldn't find Flynn. I hoped it wasn't too bold of me to explore the hallway that led to the back rooms of Arcadia. Was Flynn back there?

I suppressed a yawn. This was much later than I normally stayed up and I had to get details from Flynn. When were we leaving? What did I need to pack?

Men's voices emanated from a room on my left, its door cracked open a few inches. I eased in. Wes's broad shoulders partially blocked a shirtless Flynn.

I stopped in my tracks. I didn't mean to stare, but the man's body belonged on the pages of the graphic novels lining Arcadia's shelves. I would've bet my rental house on the perfection of his body, but I'd had no idea just how wide his shoulders were or how his biceps bunched as he held a hanger in one hand and his white suit shirt in the other.

"I'm warning you, bro, don't you dare—" Wes cut off when he noticed Flynn's alarmed stare. Wes spun around. "Tilly. Sorry we're taking so long back here."

I tried to talk, but my mouth had turned dry. I licked my bottom lip, and my belly clenched when Flynn's gaze darted to the motion. "Sorry." I started backing out. Words bubbled over like they always did when I was nervous. "I just had a few questions. I'll be missing some work, so I wanted to pack as efficiently as possible. How much food do I need to pack? Do you need my address so you can pick me up? How long of a drive—"

"Yeah, um… Yeah. I can give you the details." His gaze shifted to Wes, then back to me.

Wes sidled past me. "I'd better see what Mara needs help with."

He left but I still stood in the doorway. It wasn't like me to be speechless around Flynn, but except for the shock of seeing him the other day, we hadn't seen each other for years.

"Y-y-you'll have to drive yourself. I can message you the directions and where I put the extra key."

My heart sank. "Oh…"

Guilt flitted through his expression. "I'm working on a couple of major deals and might need to come back to the cities a couple of times."

Maybe I should come back, too, for a couple of my major clients for tutoring. I steeled my resolve. No, I deserved a darn vacation.

"As for food, they have a few gas stations, but the cabin has a full-service kitchen, so bring whatever you like to eat. I don't cook."

I barked out a laugh and he flinched. "If I didn't cook, I would've starved long ago." Clamping my mouth shut, I cursed myself for saying as much. I never talked about my childhood. Never. Long ago, I'd resolved to move forward and be the best Tilly Johnson I could be. To not bring up the past to remind myself how shitty I'd had it…then wonder what I'd done to deserve it.

He swallowed and glanced at the shirt hanging in his hands, then at me. This awkwardness was weird. Flynn had always brought out my vibrancy, but then I wasn't used to my grown woman of a body reacting so strongly to him.

And, dang it, he was trying to undress. "I'll wait outside." Stalker much? I clarified, "To give you my number."

"N-no. I mean, no need. Here." He shoved the hanger into his shirt and hung it up on a shelving unit with his tux jacket. My mouth watered as his muscles rippled with his movements. What did he do for a living again? When I'd seen him earlier in the week, he'd been wearing a suit and looking damn fine, but his body did not look like a desk jockey's.

He grabbed his phone from a shelf. "What's your number?"

I rattled if off with lightning speed. "When should I be there?"

He shrugged, and I clocked the move like a hawk. Could he pretty please go shirtless all week?

"Whenever. In the brochure, I said Sunday through Saturday."

We stared at each other for another moment. I couldn't think of another question to save my life.

If I stayed and leered at him any longer, he'd think I was creepy. "Well, okay. See you…soon." I gave him a small wave and he returned it with one I'd describe as cautious. Was he worried he'd stutter again if he spoke?

As I bounced out, I couldn't help my small smile. I'd contact my clients about my last-minute plans. Most of them had canceled earlier for the beginning of summer vacations anyway. Then I'd be free to get to know the real Flynn Halstengard.

CHAPTER 3

illy

THE POUNDING on my walls woke me up way too early for a Saturday morning. Not since I'd quit working serving jobs at twenty-four-hour diners had I been up so early on a weekend.

More pounding and a screeching noise invaded my dreams. I frowned. Was that a screwdriver?

Rolling out of bed, I grabbed a shirt and shorts from the floor to toss over the tank and undies I slept in. I padded out to my living room. Shadows moved across my drapes.

I peeked out, trying not to be noticed. Two men wearing tool belts had already set up scaffolding and were tearing away the siding at the corner of the house. A radio blared classic rock.

What the…

When I stepped out onto the landing, one of the guys noticed me. "Morning."

"Yes, it is. On a weekend. What are you guys doing here?" I kept my tone pleasant, but seriously. On a weekend?

"Sorry about that. We don't usually work Saturdays, but we're catching up on last year's hailstorm claims."

"Oh, my landlady didn't mention anything." My sweet old landlady had probably forgotten like she'd forgotten to mention when the lawn was getting treated, or when she'd let go of the snow-removal guys and I'd had to shovel my way out.

"We waited until nine to start. Did we wake you?"

It was after nine? Wow, I'd been out late, then had stayed up another two hours to pack because I'd been too wound up to sleep.

"No. It's no problem. I'm leaving town anyway." I went back inside and shut the door. I wasn't supposed to leave until tomorrow.

The pounding resumed and the radio blared. I puttered around my kitchen, preparing breakfast. The men resumed shouting instructions back and forth to each other.

Technically, today was part of my vacation. This wasn't relaxing. Once upon a time, the shouts of the men would've sent my heart racing. I would've fled the house and probably forgotten my keys and my purse.

Thanks to the adult resource center, though, I didn't feel the need to run today. I'd gotten more than my life back. They'd helped keep the experiences of my youth from haunting my days as an adult. And I'd finally gotten to pay them back.

But just because I didn't have to leave didn't mean I wanted to stay. If only I was at the cabin already. I'd planned a relaxing day at home, working the flower beds for Mrs. Blumenthal, my landlady.

I peeked out the window. Extension cords covered the lawn.

Damn. Now what? I had no money to go shopping. No cable TV. And it was too beautiful outside to watch movies all day.

My phone *pinged* from the bedroom. I rushed to check it, then grinned. Flynn. He just identified himself and gave me directions to the cabin. Aw, he'd even sent a picture of the place. The spare key was in the planter on the far right of the porch.

My lips quirked. Real original, Halstengard.

He'd said he had the cabin the whole weekend. Would he know if I went there a day early? It was either that or hang out at the library all day. I might as well grab some groceries and head there today.

I ran through the shower and braided my hair while it was still wet. Then I tossed a few last-minute toiletries into my luggage and zipped it up. Next, I tackled the food. Digging out a cooler, I calculated what I could bring with and what in my fridge would spoil in a week. All produce went into a tote bag, but I'd still need to stop at the grocery store.

I was loaded up and almost out the door when I groaned. "Mrs. Woods."

Dropping everything, I dug my phone out of my purse and dialed her first. *Get the worst over with.* The other two clients I had to notify would be completely understanding, had actually bugged me about taking a break.

Berta answered.

"Hey, it's Tilly. Is Mrs. Woods around?"

"It's your unlucky day. She just left Charlie's room, sobbing." Berta put me on hold.

My heart twisted. Poor Charlie. Maybe I should come back just to tutor him. It'd be more than a four-hour round trip, but…he would be stuck with his mother and a dubious nanny otherwise.

"Miss Johnson." Mrs. Woods sounded cool and collected.

"Mrs. Woods, I've had…something personal come up." It was a risk, not being honest, but my intuition screamed that Mrs. Woods wouldn't be supportive if she knew it was a vacation. "I have to cancel tutoring for the week. I apologize and can double up sessions next week if that works for you."

My employer sniffed. "How disappointing, Miss Johnson. You call on the weekend to cancel with so little notice?" She sighed as snidely as possible. "These things are to be expected —from you, I suppose."

What a hag. What had Mrs. Woods gone through to make her such an ugly person to those she felt were beneath her?

For the hundredth time, I had to remind myself that as long as Mrs. Woods paid me, it wasn't my concern. And I'd grown attached to Charlie. I'd put up with a lot for him.

"Thank you for understanding."

"Mmm." Mrs. Woods hung up.

I blew out a relieved breath. I made the other two calls quickly and grabbed my bags. I had new experiences all the time—out of necessity, to get away from a bad situation, or to better my life. But now, for the first time, I was embarking on an adventure without trepidation dogging my steps.

Flynn

I ROLLED MY NECK. I'd finally reached the small resort town by Lake Webber. A few more winding miles and I'd be at the cabin.

My stomach rumbled. I'd skipped lunch, thinking I didn't need it because I hadn't worked out. I'd skipped my normal run and lifting but had stopped in on a job site before leaving town.

The job site was the reason I'd left town a day early. The project manager had walked in to find me manning the Bobcat and pushing dirt around the foundation.

Since I was the boss, the manager had held his temper in check, but he'd commented, "If you do all the work on the weekend, how am I supposed to keep my crew working to earn a paycheck all week?" Insinuating that I got paid, and paid well, no matter what. Reminding me of when I'd been living paycheck to paycheck myself.

I draped a hand over the wheel. The gorgeous countryside full of leafy, green trees and rolling hills calmed me slightly. I would've felt better if I had anything to do at the cabin when I got there, but I'd purchased a new one. There'd been a rundown lake home also for sale at this same lake, but I had an aversion to living in a shithole.

But on weekends like this, when there was no work for me, I could see the appeal. I wasn't a kid anymore, and I had the time and money to work on…anything, but it was the smell. The musty, sour smell of a home that had water damage, infestations, and stains on the walls and ceilings. As soon as I stepped foot in a building that'd been neglected, I traveled back in time until I was a powerless kid who could do nothing about my situation. Maybe if I'd grown into a man who had rectified certain things about my past, it wouldn't affect me as much. But there was still one person I'd failed, one person I still let down every damn day.

Blinking away my fatigue from a restless, anxiety-filled night and a morning of getting booted off my own job site, I took the last turn to my new cabin. I let the stress drain away and tried not to remember that I'd be dunked into emotional turmoil the next day when Tulip arrived. Would she dress as pretty—normal! Not pretty. Would she dress as normal as she had last night? She'd still stuck out, dressed down for once, but I'd never noticed how silky her hair looked, probably because it was always in frizzy ponytails or swirling around her head as if she hadn't ever met the business end of a brush. But that had been over ten years ago.

I was letting out a weary sigh when the cabin came into view, along with a dark sedan parked outside the garage.

What have we here?

My heart skipped. Could Tulip be here already? No. No, that'd be ridiculous even for her.

Then again, this was Crazy J.

I parked my truck off to the side but didn't pull into the garage. In case this was an intruder or a squatter, I didn't want to alert them any more than the rumble of my diesel already had.

I slipped out of the driver's seat, leaving my bag in the cab until I got to the bottom of my mystery guest. I clicked my door shut and crept around the attached garage to the back of the cabin. I peeked in the window of the breezeway but saw nothing move. I inched open the door so it wouldn't squeak and stepped inside. Nothing was out of the ordinary. I craned my neck toward the front door. A neon-pink tote bag that could probably light the dark lake nights sat on the floor.

College kids. Don't they have their own resorts to party at? I must be getting old if the idea of a hot coed invading my getaway didn't rev my libido.

Since I was a tall man, I crouched as much as I could and tiptoed into the house, thankful I was back in Nikes instead of steel-toed work boots. Soft humming came from the kitchen. A female. Nice voice.

I straightened. A guy like me could take on female squatters and any men they brought with them. This was probably only a couple who had gotten the wrong home.

But how had they gotten in? By jimmying the locks?

I clenched my jaw and ignored the thrill that I might have something to do, like replacing the knobs. Was it possible they'd trashed the bedroom and I'd have to replace the floors or something?

The humming grew until a few words became clear. Whoever it was had a pleasant voice. Hopefully, she hadn't brought a male friend.

I entered the kitchen, my steps silent. I circled the fridge's open French doors.

A rounded ass stuck out from the opening and I grinned. What a sight. The woman kept singing and I took a moment to sweep my gaze from her ass down her long, shapely legs. Yasss… The curve of her bare back stretched my grin. Narrow straps from her bikini top hung down as she stood up and turned around.

Tulip shrieked and jumped back into the fridge.

I yelped and leaped backward. The backs of my legs hit the island and I almost rebounded into her. But I clutched the countertop behind me to steady myself.

Jars in the fridge tinkled from Tulip's impact. She gasped and spun around to steady everything. The twist in her torso drew my attention to the definition in her abs and the sleek lines of her back.

When she turned back around, I couldn't take my gaze off the Bat-Signal emblazoned across her ample breasts.

Tulip was stacked.

"T-Tulip, w-what—" I winced and dragged in a deep breath. "What are you doing here?"

Guilt crossed her expression and she wrung her hands. "Can you never call me Tulip? Never ever?"

"Why?"

31

Her gaze darted to the wall and back before her expression screwed into mild disgust. "Lots of reasons. But just Tilly. Please."

"Okay." I stared at her. Wanted her to turn around and stick her ass out again. Wanted my hand to quit twitching to cup her cheeks.

She backed away from the fridge so the doors could close. "I'm really sorry. I didn't think you'd be here until tomorrow and there were guys at my place and I've never been on vacation."

"Wait, there are men at your place?" Why did that send a surge of jealousy through my system? As if she'd been pining away for me and shunning all others for the last eleven years.

"A few. They're repairing hail damage, I guess. My landlady forgot to mention it like she forgets everything else. There was nothing else to do, I mean, in my price range, which is the library." She clamped her mouth shut as if she'd said too much.

She came a day early because of nothing to do, and I came a day early for the same reason. I never would've thought we had anything in common.

That Batman swimsuit top, though... What'd the bottoms look like? With her ass, she'd give that damn bat wings.

"Are you hungry?" she blurted. I flinched. Her volume had risen a few notches.

Was she nervous?

No, not Crazy J. She was oblivious to other people—especially what she did to me.

I drew in another calming breath, a technique Abe, my mentor, and savior, had taught me.

My stomach rumbled and she giggled. An honest to God giggle. Somehow, her threat factor diminished enough that I allowed a small smile. "I missed lunch."

"Oh!" She swiveled around and ripped open the fridge

door. "I picked up stuff for sandwiches. Nothing fancy, but I had some bread to use up or it'd be moldy by the time I got home."

I finally glanced around the kitchen. It was littered with gaudy tote bags. Her Wonder Woman tote sat on the counter beside the fridge, where it'd been blocked by the fridge doors a moment ago.

Crazy J came a day early but was making me food. So... this whole thing could be worse. She was closer to normal right now than I'd ever experienced from her before.

Her backside lured my gaze again. Her cloth shorts outlined her form perfectly and while they were black, the outline of her swim bottoms and the yellow from the Batman design were visible.

"Were you going swimming?" I blurted. Great, I was picking up her habits.

She pulled away from the fridge with an armload of food and shouldered the door shut. The meager gentleman within me that Abe had managed to save rushed to gather some of the items. Mustard, mayo, ketchup, butter. Hell, was there anything this woman hadn't packed?

I assessed everything she scattered on the table. Most of it had been opened already.

"Why didn't you just buy everything here? You didn't have to bring it all." I would've gone on a food run within an hour after I'd arrived. Could I consider this the first time a woman had bought me a meal?

"A week's worth of groceries when I already had the food? I might be wearing a Batman swimsuit, but I'm not Bruce Wayne."

But she'd spent ten grand to be here? A couple hundred in groceries shouldn't worry her.

She pulled out bread and lunch meat and—I hadn't eaten

fucking processed meat in years. I'd lose at least two of my eight abs as soon as that hit my tongue.

But my stomach insisted it was fine with whatever she was serving. I pulled out a stool and watched in fascination as she prepped our meal.

Her storm-gray eyes were serious as she assembled bread, then meat, then condiment. Thank God she had some greens to put on top, even bean sprouts. Each item she grabbed, she looked to me in question. I'd nod and she'd add it to my sandwich, except ketchup, cuz gross.

She grabbed a nearby tote and withdrew a bag of pretzels.

"Uh, no thanks." I slid the plate toward me to keep the carb load off.

"I can't have a sandwich without a side of salt." She ripped the bag open and put a handful of pretzels on her plate. Then she started constructing her sandwich.

I waited to take a bite until she was done. It was something Abe had insisted on when I'd lived with him. *Ladies first, boy.*

But this was Crazy J. Still, I couldn't do it.

She wiggled onto a stool next to me and dug in. We ate in silence and each minute that ticked by returned my stress to normal simmering levels. Would she be this mellow for the entire week?

"Do you want another?"

I jerked my gaze to her, then to her empty plate. I held the last two bites of my sandwich.

Wiping her mouth off, she scooted off her stool and went around the island to open the bread.

"N-no." I grimaced. "No, thanks." Two sandwiches when dinner was a couple of hours away? I'd have to run today after all.

Her gaze met mine and the corner of her mouth lifted. She cinched the bag and puttered around the kitchen, putting away the rest of her items. "I wasn't sure what you had for cooking capabilities here, but I brought some spaghetti and macaroni and cheese."

Pasta and processed cheese? Ick. I lost a couple more abs just thinking about them. "I'll run to town and grab some steaks. They have an awesome butcher shop. I usually grill when I'm at the lake." I didn't get away nearly as much as I should, but I'd made sure to equip the cabin with wicked grills—propane and charcoal.

"Are you sure you don't mind?" She set her hands on her hips and drew my eyes to her abdomen. She wasn't a stick. She possessed curves a man could get lost in. And she didn't seem shy about it. "This is such a nice kitchen. Like, nicer than I've ever gotten to use, but I can't…" She stopped, chewing on her lip.

"Can't what?" Weird. Usually, I wanted Crazy J—shit, *Tilly* —to stop talking, but now I hung on her dropped sentence.

"I was so busy saving to donate to the Center for Abuse Recovery that I didn't have extra for steak that wasn't discounted. I've never stepped foot in a butcher shop, but they're expensive, aren't they?" She waved it off. "That's okay. I can make myself spaghetti."

I stared at her, tallying up the comments she'd made. Landlady. Nicer kitchen than she'd ever used. Discount meat. Saving to donate?

"How long did you save for the auction?"

Pausing over the groceries, she worried her lip, and the cutest little furrow developed in her forehead. "Um…for a while. Way before the auction."

"You were going to donate anyway?"

"Yep." She resumed her organization of the kitchen. The cabin had come fully furnished and she inspected every cupboard. I didn't even know what was in here. All I ever had when I came here was beer—my vacation indulgence—

steak, and the occasional brat—no bun—if I was feeling naughty.

"How long did it take you to save the money?" I couldn't quit pressing the topic. I could've bought every bachelor at that auction and paid for all the getaways besides. But she'd lived off pasta and clearance steak to donate a specific amount.

No. Tilly wasn't going quiet now.

She continued her search. Straightening, she had a set of nested mixing bowls in her hands. "These are so cute. I have to bake something just to use them."

My mouth watered. Bake what? Brownies. I fucking loved brownies. Cake. God, could she make caramel rolls? Abe's wife had nurtured through sweets and I had gained twenty pounds after I'd moved in, even with working on the job site all day.

Tilly squatted to tuck them back in and the image seared itself into my brain. A fantasy of her in that position over me. I'd devour her.

I caught myself and grabbed the nearest bottle of water. Gulping, I smothered the lustful thoughts of my high school nightmare.

Crazy J. Crazy J. Crazy J.

Except, the longer I was around her, the less crazy she seemed. I knew nearly nothing about her beyond those three years she'd tormented me with her crush.

Wait…she hadn't answered my question. "You saved for a while then, huh?"

She stood and brushed her hair back. I wanted to run my fingers through it. "A few years, yeah. Once I got settled into a teaching job after school, then I was able to start putting it away."

"Why ten thousand two hundred and twenty-eight dollars…and fifty-five cents?"

Her gaze darted to him. "I like to be unique."

My bullshit meter went off. Super. She was supposed to show up, act like a zany sitcom reject, and drive me insane. But instead, she was leaving me a trail of breadcrumbs, and despite my no-carb discipline, I couldn't help but snatch each one up in an effort to get closer. Tilly was intriguing.

CHAPTER 4

illy

My PANIC RIPPLED like the waves on the gorgeous lake peeking through the trees. Flynn had a suspicious look in his eye like he knew I'd lied. I never fibbed. I just never got close enough to anyone to have to explain my reasons for some of the things I did. Or answer those dreaded questions about growing up. I got that not many people experienced the nightmare I had, but it didn't mean I wanted to share it.

My gaze rebounded all over the kitchen. I felt guilty as hell, all because I couldn't tell him why I'd donated the amount I had. One day, I knew I'd meet someone and grow to trust them enough with my story, but not Flynn. I didn't want to be the battered child around him. The blond, built, walking fantasy was my escape. What daydreams would I have to get lost in if I lost the one of Flynn?

"Want to give me the grand tour?" I asked brightly.

His light brows popped up. Subtlety wasn't my strength. I scurried out of the kitchen, hoping he would follow.

"Where should I put my bags?" Retrieving mine from by the front door, I spun around and hit a wall of man chest.

"Tu—Tilly."

I tipped my head back. He was so much taller than I remembered. He'd had a growth spurt after I'd dropped out. "What?" I squeaked.

He gazed down at me, concern in his emerald irises. I wanted to cry with frustration. How many years had I wished to make Flynn feel more than flustered? But I didn't want his worry. Like I didn't want his pity. I couldn't win, and he was starting to make me feel like Tulip Johnson. That was a place I couldn't go back to. A shudder ran through me.

"Did I say something wrong?"

Damn, he'd noticed. "No. I…" Lying hadn't gotten me anywhere, so I'd spare him a kernel of truth. "I don't like talking about myself."

Those lust-inducing lips of his curled into a smile. "Then it'll be a long week if you have to listen to me prattle on about work."

We stood less than a foot apart, but neither one moved. "What is it you do? Mara said you were in construction."

Pride highlighted his features and it looked good on him. Before, much to my chagrin, I'd thought he'd looked arrogant. "Corporate construction. I own my own business."

"Wow." Some people had it all. Logically, I knew he'd worked for it, but…I'd worked pretty damn hard, too, and this cabin blew away any place I'd ever lived. But he probably hadn't had loser parents to overcome.

"I built Arcadia."

"That place is gorgeous," I breathed.

Little lines crinkled at the corners of his eyes and my

belly clenched. One tiny imperfection that made him suddenly human and attainable.

He was still so close, the heat of his body surrounded me in a cocoon I never wanted to leave. In high school, I'd chatted with him, always on his heels. He always had to be somewhere in those days. It was nice that he had slowed down now, even for just a moment.

"It's one of my favorites." His voice had dropped low, husky.

"I'm sure it helped that your client was your best friend."

"My best friend's wife. The place is hers. She made him keep his hands off."

"What else have you built?" I swayed closer, the distance between us shrinking to bare inches.

His gaze dipped to my cleavage and I should've died a little that he'd caught me in a swimsuit I'd never usually wear. But Mara had given me a deal and I had walked out with three swimsuits for the price of one.

His gaze licked up my neck and I shivered. Another move that didn't escape his notice. He caressed my cheek with the backs of his fingers.

"Cold?"

"No," I whispered.

He dropped his gaze to my lips and his head bent.

Ohgodohgodohgod. My eyelids drifted shut and my lips parted.

He hovered over my mouth but didn't touch me. I opened my eyes as he straightened.

He cleared his throat and spun around. "Your room. I forgot, sorry."

So it was like that. I snagged his elbow and stalked in front of him. I was so not missing this opportunity.

Grabbing his face in both hands, I rose to my toes and smashed my mouth on his.

He stumbled back in surprise until his back hit the front door, but then he snaked his arms around me. His lips went from tense with surprise to supple under mine. Within a second, he took control and kissed me back until he stole my breath. Palms flat on my ass, he pulled me flush against him. To save my balance, I circled my arms around his shoulders.

Oh yes. His tongue swept in and I opened for him. He was heat, man, and lingering sandwich. I rocked into him, anything to ease the quivering in my sex his kiss caused.

His arousal grew between us, a hard length as big as my imagination.

Who's a lucky girl? I deepened the kiss, causing my belly to rub against his erection.

He jolted, his head flinging back and hitting the door.

"Ow, damn." His firm grip was now on my upper arms as he sidled out and around me.

Once he let go, I pressed my fingers to my temple. My head was spinning! He kissed even better than I'd fantasized. But he was uncomfortable, for whatever reason. I tried not to be offended, but I would've been just fine letting things run their course right here against the door. On the floor. I didn't care.

"Well, we got that over with," I said it more to cover the hurt that he'd pushed me away. Had I done something wrong? None of my exes had ever complained.

His brow furrowed, and he swung his gaze back toward me.

I shrugged. His gaze flickered like he was going to check out my cleavage again but didn't.

"It seemed like we were going to and then you almost walked away, so I got it over with."

"Got it over with," he echoed.

Bobbing my head like this was an ordinary conversation,

I smiled. "Yep. Now you can show me my room and I can go dip a toe in the lake."

"And I'll go grab my protein for the week." He frowned. "Steaks. I eat meat for protein."

"I gathered that. You must work out." I shot him a wicked smile, but he looked as dazed as before. Always with the awkwardness. "Have a good drive."

I hitched my luggage and breezed past him, but when I got to the hall by the stairs, he said, "The sleeping areas are in the upper level."

Changing course, I muscled my luggage to the first stair, but it was lifted out of my hands. The way Flynn jogged up the stairs, his jean shorts snug around his epic ass, the suitcase didn't weigh as much for him as it did for me.

I followed him to the landing at the top. Three doors surrounded a seating area. Slowing down, I did a one-eighty. What a beautiful setting to plan tutoring lessons. The logs gave it a rustic appeal, but the plush carpet was soft enough to sleep on. The chairs were all overstuffed and faced the railing that overlooked the rest of the cabin. The beams that arched across the ceiling looked close enough to swing on.

"This place is breathtaking."

I got no reply. Treading along the path Flynn's shoes had left in the carpet, I peeked in each room. One was a bathroom with—

"Oh my God, is that a jetted tub?" Flipping on the light as I charged in and gasped. "It is!" I clapped and jumped up and down.

Flynn finally appeared in the doorway of what must be my room. "It's small, though."

"Are you serious? Small is a bucket to wash out of. This is heaven." Hopefully, he took that as a random comparison and not a literal one. Technically, it'd been a basin.

I turned the light off and went to the door Flynn wasn't

standing in. "Your room?" Not waiting for his answer, I walked inside. "Whoa. Everything in this place is so nice. You even have your own bathroom? How many bathrooms does this place have?"

"Three. And there's a hot tub on the back deck, but I have to get it ready."

I sucked in a breath, otherwise, I was going to squeal and I knew he didn't handle that well. "You better not be lying."

He gave me a steady look. "It's just a hot tub."

The kitchen. The tubs. The whole stinking cabin. He owned his own business.

"You're rich, aren't you?"

Some high schools were in better neighborhoods than others. The one I'd gone to had never been about personal wealth, but there had been a ton of wealthy kids, several that had made my school life hell. I'd never realized he was one of them.

"I do all right."

The look I passed him had to be droll. "'All right' isn't a small jetted tub and a hot tub on the deck of your *vacation home*." When his expression turned guarded, I clarified. "There's nothing wrong with having money. It's about perspective. I've never sat in either tub." For a long time, I'd barely had a pot to piss in—literally. "I've never had a fridge the size of my car. I've never owned my own home, much less two. And that's okay, too."

He cocked his head, but I kept going.

"I've never been to the lake before, either. To you, this might be a normal getaway, just a typical break in your routine, but this is my first vacation ever. I'm very glad I get to have all these new experiences and to do it with someone I know." Not alone, like I'd always been.

When the words had spilled out, they felt right. But he was gaping at me.

43

Enough chitchat. I had brownies to bake, a lake to swim in, two tubs to relax in, and only seven more days to do it in.

Flynn

I HAULED her bag into her room. As the list of things Tilly hadn't done grew longer and longer, I had felt smaller and smaller. She'd always been the wacky girl who lusted after me. Now she was becoming a person, one clearly better than me, though that wouldn't be hard. She was a special education teacher. As soon as she heard about what I'd done after graduation, she'd think I was the lousiest human to have walked the earth.

I was about to castrate myself for that kiss, and it didn't matter if my hands still begged to be filled with her flesh.

Where'd she learned to kiss like that? No hesitation, no coyness—full throttle, like the girl herself.

Just as that thought was completed, she hooked her thumbs in her waistband and dropped her shorts.

My breath froze. Long legs kicked the shorts away. I wanted to lick my way up her body and wrap them around my waist. Her swim bottoms were cute as fuck with the matching top, and the combo set her gray eyes sparkling.

She looked around and spotted the bag I'd set on the luggage rack.

I should leave, but she was going to go digging in that bag and my feet wouldn't move.

Dayum. The erection that had finally flagged roared back to life. She bent over the bag to retrieve something from inside and I stared at her ass the whole time.

With other women, I'd know they were doing this on

purpose, but Tilly seemed absolutely unaware of the effect she had. She straightened and reached back to gather her hair.

I suppressed a groan. In the full-length mirror on the opposite wall, her breasts rose with her arms in the air, and I stood riveted the entire time she gathered her hair into a messy bun.

"Is there a path to the lake?"

I couldn't answer right away. How hard would it be to crowd her back to the bed and rip that suit off with my teeth? One flick of my wrist and I'd be buried in that wet heat.

Her head tilted. "Are you okay?" She glided toward me, her hand going for my forehead. "You look flushed. You aren't running a fever, are you?"

I caught her wrist—and found myself in the same damn position as earlier when I'd been about to kiss her. It was even harder to remember why I shouldn't.

"Flynn?" Her eyes grew wide. She swallowed hard, her gaze glued to my hand.

My name should've been a cold splash of reality, but it was her reaction. I loosened my grip.

Fuck, nothing I was doing was working. I could move out for the week, but that would negate the bachelor contract and be rude as hell.

"I'm trying to stay away from you," I said instead.

She opened her mouth, then closed it. Her lips turned down. "Do you want to?"

"No." I snarled the word. "You had such a big fucking crush on me in school—I wasn't going to lead you on."

"But you want me?"

"Yes." I still gripped her arm, but my thumb caressed her skin.

"Did you want me then?"

Some of my aggression eased. "No."

Her arm went limp and I let it go. Ah, hell. I'd hurt her feelings.

She glanced away. "You were always awkward around me. I didn't know it was because you didn't like me."

Okay, this was working. This was creating distance between us. I'd keep going as much as it hurt me. "I called you Crazy J."

Her eyes flared, first with shock and then hurt. "I...I... didn't know."

"You seemed like a nutcase, Tulip, but I don't think you are. Why?"

"Don't call me that!"

Her venomous tone pushed me back a step. "It was your name. Why'd you change it?"

"Because I never liked it." She cradled her arm to herself. I hadn't grabbed her hard, but from the faraway look in her eye, the action only symbolized the upheaval in her mind. Then she slanted me a look. "Crazy J, really?"

I chuckled. "You sounded a little wacky when you had your jaw wired shut." She made a choking sound and I grew somber. "It's okay, Tilly. We're all awkward as kids."

"Awkward doesn't describe braces as a teenager."

"You did pick neon pink and yellow."

She shifted her gaze to look out the window and lifted a shoulder. "Go big or go home, right?"

Her tone was flat. I'd expected her to own her jaw surgery and brilliant braces. They'd fit her whole look back then. What else would her motivation have been?

She was staring out the window. Blue glittered in the distance. I didn't want to leave, but I'd get the supply run over with so I could...what? Watch her? Hang with her?

"Do you know how to swim?" Yeah, that was why I was in a hurry to get back. Didn't want Tilly drowning while I was perusing prime cuts of steak. My heart rate kicked up at the thought.

"No. Why? I won't go out far."

"Then wait until I get back from town." She was about to argue but I shushed her with a finger on her lips. Bad decision. Too soft, too plump, too tempting. I snatched my hand away. "Test the jets on this tub and I'll get the hot tub running tonight after you check out the lake."

Her pink tongue darted out to lick where my finger had been. She was going to kill me.

"Fine," she grumbled, but the Tilly light was back in her eyes.

For a second, I thought of hanging around to see if she'd strip out of her bikini in front of me as she had with her shorts.

I turned on my heel and made a beeline for the front door. How was I going to survive a week without touching her?

Tilly

I LAID my laptop next to me on the seat. It was useless. A blond-haired, green-eyed bachelor was clogging too many of my thought processes. My lesson plans would have to wait. I was on vacation.

When would Flynn get back? Would he take his time?

The kiss had made him so skittish. I'd had no clue why, but he'd certainly filled me in.

Crazy J.

They had called me that? I couldn't argue. As an adult, I was nothing but honest with myself, but I'd sugarcoated some parts of growing up. Tears pricked my eyes. Nope, every minute of it had sucked.

At least Flynn hadn't shunned me outright. I might not have survived the humiliation.

Hadn't there been any part of him that had been just a teeny bit interested?

Jaw wired shut.

Nope. I could see that clearly now. No wonder I hadn't dated until college—and I'd even started college a year later than normal.

I rubbed my eyes and stretched. Flynn had suggested a bath, but I wasn't wasting the water if I was going into the lake. I'd luxuriate in the jets afterward.

But that didn't mean I had to sit around and wait for a guy, even if that guy was my dream man. I rubbed my wrist. When he'd grabbed it, adrenaline had flooded my veins. Lingering survival instincts. But his expression had been more panicked, nothing close to the rage I'd seen in my dad's eyes.

I tucked my computer away. Yes, a walk was a good idea. Waiting for Flynn to get back before I did anything was something my mom would've done. Probably still did. I wouldn't know, hadn't talked to them for over twelve years, and didn't want to.

Taking the stairs, I evaluated my outfit. I'd thrown the shorts back on and a pair of flip-flops, but I only planned a walk, not a hike. This should be fine. The yellow bat wings across my breasts lifted my mood. I would've never walked around home with just a swim top, but once Flynn had seen me in it, why bother to be embarrassed? Just because I never showed off my body didn't mean I was ashamed of it. Clothes were a necessity. I' never had the money for them to be fashionable.

I'd love to wear more clothing that would incite Flynn's

reaction. He'd always acted stunned around me, unsure of what to say or do, but today had been different. The look in his eye when I'd caught him staring at my breasts or my stomach…

I grinned. Day one of this vacation had started out awesome.

Warm air enveloped me as soon as I stepped outside. I toed along the stone path that ended at a narrow trail down to the lake.

A low laugh of delight escaped. A dock! Walk first, soak the toesies later.

Leaves rustled around me as a gentle breeze blew off the lake. The air cooled me off. In a couple of months, it'd be hot and muggy, but at the beginning of June, the wind was perfect.

A girl could get used to this. I closed my eyes and inhaled a slow breath. Stress rolled off me in waves as I imagined it dripping off my fingertips. How had I not realized how tense I'd been? For so many years. I couldn't remember a time I hadn't lived under a mountain of stress and anxiety. Meals were no longer an uncertain event, but I had to work hard to provide them and I only had myself to worry about.

Not true. I fretted terribly over my kids, both those in my class and the ones I tutored. Anxious thoughts plagued me constantly about being able to maintain the level of clients I needed for tutoring. I adored teaching, but my dream was to open my own business, one designed solely for one-on-one tutoring, and I wanted to fundraise and develop grants to make it affordable for all families.

I'd been so busy worrying about my hopes and dreams tanking—and watching where I stepped on the rough sandy shore with only my sandals—that when I looked up, I was already on another cabin's property.

Oops. I turned around. Flynn's cabin and even his dock

weren't visible from where I stood. On the way back, I closed my eyes and lifted my face to the sun. Spending my vacation worrying wasn't going to help anything. I had to relax and table my thoughts for a few days, but my lifelong habit of planning for the future was more a survival instinct and harder to set aside.

A man's voice drifted on the wind. I hoped I hadn't intruded on another couple's lake getaway.

I opened my eyes before I veered into the water. Flynn came jogging around the bend, his gait relaxed but his face tense.

"Tilly. Fuck, you scared me." He stopped in front of me.

"Why in the world were you scared about me?" No one cared about me.

My throat grew thick as that statement echoed in my head. Sometimes, no matter how hard I tried to maintain my optimism, my true feelings emerged.

"I got back and the cabin was empty. You said you didn't know how to swim but I couldn't find you outside, either." He glanced around. The water was to my right, trees to my left, and another plush cabin at my back. "What were you doing?"

He'd been worried about me. Best vacation *ever*. "I ran out of sugar and thought I'd ask these nice folks if they could loan me some." I grinned and playfully punched him on the shoulder. "I was just going for a walk before I sat on the dock and hung my feet in. But now that you're here, I can go wading."

I continued on the path and he fell into step beside me. I peppered him with questions about what he'd bought, what I should cook with it if we could go fishing. He muttered that he didn't have a boat and glowered at the path in front of us.

He went from relieved to sullen. Had I done something wrong? Had the sandwich worn off? Was he hangry now?

I brushed it off. The lake beckoned. I shed my sandals and shorts. Small rocks bit into my feet as I jumped and danced into the water.

"Oh my god, it's cold," I squealed but kept plowing in. Giggles escaped as the waves lapped higher on my legs, sending shivers rippling over my body. I threw my head back and laughed with pure delight.

The lake bottom wasn't any more comfortable on my feet than the shore, but I managed to wobble around.

Flynn was staring at me, his hands shoved in his pockets, as still as a statue.

"Are you coming in?" I glided my hands around, letting cool water slide through my fingers. I was only halfway down the length of the dock, the water to the tops of my thighs. My feet were visible.

His throat worked like he was going to speak, but he just shook his head.

"What's wrong?"

His gaze dipped to my belly. "Nothing. I need to start the grill."

Then why didn't he? He didn't move. "Oh, but you're acting as my lifeguard and can't until I'm done." I held up two fingers. "Two more minutes."

He gave me a curt nod.

I might've pushed it to five minutes, even ten, as I frolicked in the water. The only thing warding off a chill from the cool water was the heat of his gaze licking across me. He was either taking his lifeguarding duties seriously, or I was getting to him. I waded back to shore and grinned to myself. The mighty Flynn might just find me attractive.

CHAPTER 5

lynn

I WATCHED as much as I could stand of Tilly exiting the water like a nymph in the sexiest Batman bikini ever made. My cock was weeping for just one touch of her skin, and every giggle she let loose banged around my body until I could barely stop myself from stripping down and charging in after her.

How the hell had Crazy J with the neon braces become that damn sexy?

How the hell could I be lusting after her that badly? I'd been with a lot of women. In high school, I'd slept with girls who were cheerleaders, on the dance team, even gymnasts. And I'd fucked them all as adults. Picked them up wearing clothing that could just as well be see-through, stripped it off, had sex, and walked away.

Tilly should just be another girl. No, she wasn't. She was

Tulip "Crazy J" Johnson. I should not lose one drop of blood to my cock for her. But I couldn't argue with how appealing she was. Without the wacky wear, she was sweet in a magnetizing way. Without the odd choice in fashion, she was sexy as hell, but it was her uninhibited joy that was as addicting as an eight ball.

Was it the whole reverse-psychology thing? I couldn't have her and that made her so damn irresistible?

Yeah. Yeah, that made sense. And she wanted me, too, but she wasn't coy or using her body as a lure to hook me. I was used to the game, the one played in the clubs to pick up ladies. They'd give me "the look" and I'd strike up a conversation. I'd tell them only enough to keep them interested. Business owner was usually enough. I always made sure to say nothing that resembled a promise for the future. Then it was my place or theirs, and I always opted for theirs if at all possible. Sometimes they had a roommate and I'd just grin wickedly. Deal, done. The next morning, I might go for another round before I walked out.

But Tilly wasn't playing any games. She was herself, she liked me, and we were stuck together all week. I couldn't handle another full day of her prancing around half-dressed and giggling, much less suffer through seven more days. Well, there was Monday—I'd have to run in and meet with John.

I strode up the deck, past the grill, toward the sliding glass door into the kitchen, and froze. Behind me, visible in the reflected glass, Tilly crested the stairs, her breasts swaying in their top, her long legs sparkling with droplets. Her sandals and shorts were in one arm and her eyes glowed with elation.

So. Damn. Beautiful.

I couldn't do this. It wasn't like me to ignore my body's needs and it thought it needed Tilly hard and fast. But she was a teacher. Of special-needs kids. I couldn't start a relationship.

Relationships meant honesty and if I was honest, she'd think I was the worst person in the world. And she'd be right.

While I was stuck in the mental dilemma between touching her or tying my hands to my sides, she passed, opened the door, and slipped into the house, calling back that she'd shower and help with supper.

So now I had to cook while she was naked upstairs. I vibrated with the urge to stalk her and slake my lust.

She wanted me, had for years. I'd wanted her all of one fucking day and could barely stand it.

What if I gave us what we both wanted...and made sure it sucked?

I'd take the edge off, she'd be disappointed and lose the mystery of me, and I'd convince myself she was just another lay.

My body screamed "yes" at the excuse to touch her and before my mind could point out how wrong it was, I blew in through the door, barely remembering to close it to keep the bugs out.

I sped up the stairs. Her door wasn't completely shut and I pushed it open—and nearly came to a full halt. My steps slowed as I approached her.

Naked. In all her glory. She'd stripped off the suit. Her eyes went wide in shock and she covered her bare, spectacular breasts, but her breath hitched at my expression.

"Flynn."

"We need to do this." My voice was guttural. If she said no, I'd throw myself out the window to keep from touching her. My gaze dropped to her sex. My erection throbbed so hard I feared I'd lose my load just putting the condom on.

"Okay." She dropped her hands.

"Get on the bed." Make it bad. Make it bad. At least for

her. Once I stroked through her folds, my intuition said I'd be lost. I dug my wallet out and grabbed a condom. There was a whole box in the other room.

I could make it good, take her all week, and then make the sex lousy.

No! I had to do this wrong the first time.

She crawled back onto the bed, her legs splayed, opening herself to me.

Yesss. She wasn't completely bare like some women I'd been with, and honestly, I didn't care. Tilly was perfect, her curls glistening for me.

Her gaze wandered over me, from the fly of my shorts to the condom in my hand. Now that I had her right where I'd fantasized about her since that damn auction, it was hard to go fast. Her body was ripe for savoring, for pleasuring until she begged, licking and caressing for hours while I brought her to climax over and over again.

The condom shook in my fingers.

Make it bad. Break the spell between us. This was for her more than me.

I ripped the packet open. Damn. I was fully dressed. The shorts were first, shoved down in seconds, and I was caught in her stormy gaze as I rolled the condom on.

Her eyes went wide again as she eyed my length. I liked her attention on me way too much.

The condom was settled, and I kneeled on the bed in between her legs. She propped herself on her elbows, her knees up, her expression wondrous.

She was going to kill me.

I should kiss her first or something. Then her lush breasts would smash against my chest. If I kissed her mouth, I'd have to tongue those nipples. How sweet would her creamy center be?

It wouldn't be making things worse for her if I got lost in

pleasuring her. No more touching than necessary. Hands on her knees, I shoved them wide. "Ready?"

She bit her lip. Her hips rolled toward me, but she glanced from my cock to my mouth. Was she going to insist we be more intimate? Would I be able to deny her?

Like me, she seemed ready to go from zero to sixty. She nodded.

I placed myself at her entrance. Her sex surrounded the tip of my shaft, her flesh greedy, but I wasn't a complete bastard. I was after shitty sex, but she wasn't as wet and ready as I would normally ensure, so there would be no rabid thrusting.

I pushed forward, just enough to envelope the tip. She groaned and rocked her pelvis and I couldn't stop until I was buried.

My thoughts faltered. Her body was heaven. A hot furnace gripped my dick and her muscles massaged my length. I could climax just seated inside of her.

"Flynn, you can't imagine how long I've wanted this."

Her words were a cold splash of reality. I couldn't encourage this thing between us. I had to crush her crush. She was too... for everything. Too good, too sweet, too innocent. I wasn't worthy.

I rocked out and back in. My climax was almost at the peak, her tight sex, and soft moans the most erotic thing I'd experienced, and I just let it happen. I allowed my body to get carried away faster than ever before without seeing to her orgasm. Even a weak orgasm was still an orgasm. Make it bad.

I threw my head back and as much as my body screamed at me not to, I withdrew and shook my release outside of her.

She let out a gasp when I slid out and I was afraid to open

my eyes and face her. My first time hadn't even been as epically terrible as this.

But I looked at her. She seemed disoriented and confused as she contemplated the space between her legs. I pushed off the bed. She closed her knees and let them fall to the side.

I slapped the side of her ass. "Good game."

Covering my disdain at my actions, I gave her my back and left her room.

After I shut the door to the master bath, I leaned my forehead against the wood. My body shook, all the adrenaline and self-loathing draining out. Simmering lust I feared would never go away stayed with me, leaving me half hard.

That was supposed to have been the worst sex of my life. Instead, the wet heat of her body had gotten me off in less than a minute and we hadn't so much as kissed. But my lips remembered how supple she'd been when I'd kissed her earlier. Or when she'd kissed me.

Tilly worked me up tighter than Crazy J. This was so much worse than high school.

~

Tilly

MY SEX THROBBED, plainly stating I hadn't been brought to completion.

Warm water bubbled around me in the jetted tub. Funny, I'd assumed I'd be more thrilled to use it. Instead, I soaked and debated whether to make myself come or hope that Flynn would do it later. If there was a later.

A little swirl of excitement snaked through me. I'd had sex with Flynn Halstengard.

The feeling crashed. And it'd been *awful.*

Not, like, *all* of it. For a few seconds when he'd been moving inside of me, he'd fulfilled all my fantasies. He was the only guy on earth who didn't have to do more to get me off. Maybe it was his superpower, holding that power over all women. But it had been over and done before I could say "orgasm."

Did he have sex like that with everyone? I wasn't delusional. A man who looked like him had to have sex a lot. A man who walked like him, smiled like him, talked like him, had to be confident in his own body—and with his skills in the sack. He looked like the superhero of sex.

I sighed. I'd been spending too much time in Arcadia, gotten a little too lost in the graphic novels I picked up for the kids. I should know—all superheroes had a weakness, and either I was it or he was terrible at sex.

Enough. I yanked the drain and stood, water sluicing off my body. A tremor ran up my spine. When he'd kneeled and shoved my knees apart… My core quivered. I wanted more of that. Maybe he'd been too…something. The way he'd charged into my room and announced we should have sex? Something was going on with him.

One more chance.

I dried off and dressed in my pajamas—blue flimsy shorts with white stars and a red tank top with the Wonder Woman insignia. Mara had started selling clothing in Arcadia, and she gave me awesome deals on all of it, not just the swimsuits.

I wouldn't be going out again tonight, and Flynn had already seen me naked.

I'd had sex with Flynn. And I didn't miss the curl of disappointment when I thought of it.

Steeling myself, I trotted downstairs, but Flynn was out on the deck, manning the grill, his rigid shoulders toward me.

Finding fresh veggies on the counter that he must've picked up on his trip to town, I prepped a salad, then toasted some garlic bread.

The sliding door opened, but as the silence stretched, I turned to see what was wrong. Paused in the doorway, Flynn hastily looked away and carried the plate of steaming steaks to the kitchen.

"Hope you're hungry," he said, presenting me with his epic ass. All that protein did him *gooood*.

The aroma of the food teased my nose. This was almost as nice as eating out. Unless I was on a date, that never happened.

We settled at the table, Flynn taking the far side.

Okay. Hurt lingered that he didn't choose the chair next to me, but I wasn't up to interpreting his actions. The day had already been filled with new experiences, all made a tad overwhelming by the man across from me.

I bit into the first cut of steak. Savory flavor burst over my taste buds and I closed my eyes and groaned.

Flynn's silverware clattered against his plate. My eyes popped open, but he'd recovered and was slicing his steak.

More for conversation than interest, I asked, "What cut of meat is this?"

"Ribeye."

"It's good."

"Thanks."

We ate in silence. He didn't touch the bread but ate up most of the salad.

Before he had a chance to clear the table and run, I peppered him with questions. "How'd you get into construction?"

His jaw clenched for a heartbeat before he answered. "My dad was a carpenter."

"You're a business owner in your twenties. Did you follow

your dad around, then take over for him?" There had to be a fascinating story, and Flynn seemed like a guy who'd relish telling it.

He pushed his plate away, his expression blank. "His boss hired me on and it took off from there."

I waited, but he didn't elaborate. "What type of construction?"

"I build corporate spaces."

"There must be a lot more to that than houses."

He nodded, still reserved. "I used to build houses."

"How'd you make the jump?"

He lifted a shoulder. "It just happened. Houses got bigger, I got talking with the owners... Where'd you go in high school?"

I recoiled at the sudden subject change. He hit on a time in my life I never talked about, which was most of my life. I answered honestly, my irritation at his vague answers eating at me. "I dropped out."

His surprised gaze flew up. "What? Really?"

"Yep. Got my GED instead." Now that I'd opened the door, I had no wish to step through it. My Wonder Woman pajamas weren't lending me any more girl power than I normally had. Standing, I gathered a bunch of dishes to carry to the counter.

He did the same. "Why?"

"I just made the decision and it took off from there." How would he feel, having his own words flung back at him?

"You started college early then?"

"No, a year late, actually." Ack. I was worse at this game than he was.

"What happened?" He shadowed me around the kitchen, putting everything away.

"Life happened." I spun and started. He was right in front of me, his body blocking out everything. "I'm sure you know how it goes." He must if he didn't offer any of his personal history for me.

"Is that when you changed your name?"

"Close." I exhaled and rubbed the side of my head. The filling, delicious dinner wasn't enough to stave off the headache talking about my past brought on. "I'm sorry, Flynn. I don't like to talk about it."

He replaced my hand with his own, one on each side of my head. His thumbs massaged my temples.

Oh, that was nice. His strong hands were gentle. Couldn't he have done this earlier in my bedroom?

Abruptly, he stopped and stepped back. "I'll let you rest then. Good night."

He was out of the kitchen before I could blink. I peeked at the time on the microwave. It wasn't even eight p.m. Looked like I'd have time to plan my lessons after all.

Best vacation ever.

illy

I SWUNG my feet in the cool water. I was perched at the end of the dock. The sun was high overhead, warming the tops of my shoulders as I frowned into the clear lake.

Sundays were usually a quiet day, but this was ridiculous. Flynn had stayed in his room all day. We'd said hi over breakfast, then he'd disappeared into his room. I'd been about to knock to let him know I had made lunch, but his voice on the other side of the door had persuaded me to leave him alone. He must be working on vacation, too.

I kicked my feet and watched them glide through the waves, releasing my frustration with the effort. Sure, I'd brought work with me, but I didn't do it when he was around. It just seemed kinda rude.

But I wasn't the owner of a multimillion-dollar business.

As more hours passed, the excuse didn't make me feel better.

With a sigh, I drew my feet up and stood. I shed my shorts and T-shirt. Today's swimsuit was one Mara hadn't had to talk me into. The front was a red-and-black checkerboard pattern, and the back was half red, half black. While the suit wasn't an obvious superhero design, it was cool as hell. Mara had invited me to the next Twin Cities Comic-Con, and I planned to dress up as Harley Quinn. To my students' delight, I had the laugh perfected.

I evaluated the water. It was deep enough to jump in, but not so deep that I might find myself sinking because I couldn't swim. But I could float and the dock was right there.

The responsible thing to do would be to use the shore to enter the water, but I wasn't looking forward to treading over the rocks again. I narrowed my eyes. Going inside to ask Flynn to lifeguard for me wasn't an option. Besides, I'd gone swimming in the community center. I would jump in and grasp the sides of the dock, and besides, it probably wasn't terribly deep this close to shore. How much depth did a fishing boat need anyway?

Steeling myself, I squeezed my eyes shut and jumped.

With a splash, I cannonballed to the bottom. My toes hit the mud and I pushed back up. Sputtering at the surface, I blew out water and doggie paddled to the dock.

Rhythmic pounding startled me and my hand slipped off the slick wood. I submerged. Again, I rebounded off the bottom and cleared the surface.

"What the hell do you think you're doing?"

I almost lost my hold again. Flynn loomed over me, his green eyes flashing with fury. I looked from him to the cabin. Had he seriously run out here from his room that fast? It'd been less than thirty seconds since I'd made contact with the water.

"I'm playing in the lake." I sounded defensive. I was defensive. What I'd done wasn't a good idea, but what else was there to do but work?

He rested his hands on his lean hips. "By yourself?"

"It's my vacation."

"What would you have done i-i-if—dammit! Only you ever make me stutter again." He shoved a hand through his hair and turned around, then spun back like he was afraid to take his eyes off me.

"I'm sorry?"

"Yeah. You should be."

I drew back at his adamant tone. Oh, no he *didn't*. I pulled myself along the dock until my feet touched. "You should be, too. If you want to work while you're here, fine. I'm going out of my mind with boredom, and I've already put in a few hours of lesson planning. If I'd known I'd be sitting on my ass alone in the woods, I would've planned some things to do."

Anger churned in his gaze, then died. "What would you plan?"

I blinked at his abrupt change in demeanor. "This. I was close enough to the dock. Hiking. I've always wanted to hike through nature. Maybe tomorrow I'll run in and grab some brochures for nature trails close by. Then there's fishing. I've never fished before."

"Do you have a license?"

"I need a license?" My heart sank. I wanted to fish. "Do they cost money?"

"I'll get you one."

"Oh no. You're already paying for this whole week."

He cast me a droll look. "You paid for it."

"Sort of, but you bought the food."

He snorted. "Not nearly as much as you brought." He glanced at the cabin and paused, his expression contemplative. "Look, I need to run into work tomorrow. We'll cross one thing off your list today if you promise to stay out of the lake while I'm gone. Then Tuesday, we'll do another. Think of one for each day."

He'd be gone all day Monday? Disappointment soured my outlook. Oh well. I was used to being alone.

"Tilly? That sound okay?"

What could I say? *You let me down in bed yesterday, you've ignored me all day, and now you're not even going to be here all of Monday.* "Sure. Where are the instructions for the hot tub? I can get it cleaned out tomorrow while you're gone."

A muscle jumped in his jaw as he stared at me. "Finish your swim and I'll start on the hot tub when you're done."

I jumped up and down with excitement, in slo-mo, thanks to the water. His gaze dropped to where my breasts bounced in the water. I couldn't help the big grin as I fell backward. Water closed over my head and I bobbed back to the surface.

"Don't!" His hands fisted on his hips in frustration. "Fuck. Don't do that to me."

I wiped my eyes clear. "This is only, like, four feet deep right here."

His expression clouded. "I don't care, all right? Accidents happen."

"Can you swim, Flynn?"

"Yes."

"Then why are you so afraid for me?"

He ground his teeth. "Like I said, accidents happen."

Everything in me went still. "Who did the accident happen to?"

He flinched and looked away. I didn't think he'd answer, but he spoke low. "My sister."

My mouth dropped open and I gasped. "I'm so sorry." I moved as fast as I could to shore. I'd just given the poor man a heart attack, no clue he'd suffered such a tragedy.

"No. Please." He followed along with me down the dock. "You don't have to get out."

I adopted my most reassuring expression. "I can't relax and swim when I make you worry so much. Don't worry. The lake will be here Tuesday. I'll help you with the hot tub."

"There's not much you can help with. Why don't you start dinner?"

"You'll have to show me how to grill."

He leveled me with a steady stare. "You think you're man enough to learn?"

I barked a laugh and made my voice nasally. "I've got the chest hair to prove it, Puddin'."

"Pud— Oh, your swimsuit."

Delighted he got the reference, I exited the water and stepped gingerly over the rocks. "I should've gotten swim shoes instead of swimsuits."

"No. The suits were, uh…a good choice." He pivoted and walked back down the dock. A small smile crept over my mouth when he stooped to grab my things. The fluid way his body moved… Last night had to have been a fluke.

I waited for him as he retrieved my sandals. After I stepped into them, we walked to the cabin. He ran through instructions on the grill and we decided on bun-less burgers.

"What's with you and carbs?" I'd never have believed it until now, but he could be…uptight.

"I don't work out just to cover my muscles in a layer of fat."

"You don't enjoy working out?"

His expression shifted like he didn't understand the question. "Does anyone?"

"I do. I mean, I've never belonged to a gym, but I go for walks, I run sometimes. The library has a nice collection of workout DVDs. It's fun to try different ones." I laughed at myself. "It made me come to terms with my coordination or lack of. Have you found something you enjoy?"

His eyes heated, and I knew exactly what he enjoyed. And I wanted to, with him, so much.

"I liked building houses," he finally said.

"Then why don't you?"

"I've got people for that."

"But you enjoy it."

"But I'm the boss. Someone has to be in charge."

Weird. Had he taken over a company because he'd had to and not because he'd wanted to? I would have asked, but I didn't feel like a repeat of last night's minimalist conversation.

"So, there ya go," he said abruptly, gesturing to the grill. "I'll get the hot tub going. Just, uh, go ahead and stay in that swimsuit for it."

He marched off the deck. I gave myself a silent high five and turned to the food. Could tonight be the night Flynn opened up with me some more?

Flynn

I willed the tub to fill as fast as possible. I should pat myself on the back for coming out last weekend and cleaning it.

Tilly was at the grill, preparing way too much food. *Gotta set you up with protein, Puddin'.* God, that drove me crazy. Every time she used that fake falsetto, I had to restrain myself from dragging her down to the nearest flat surface, moving that flimsy strip of fabric aside, and plunging into her heat. Would she be ready for me that fast? Cuz I sure as fuck was ready for her.

Was she even still interested after I'd pulled my disappearing act? Then I'd barely talked to her over dinner and ignored her, unintentionally, all day.

But I'd been watching her like a creepy stalker. I'd heard her go outside and I'd abandoned my laptop to watch her lush body saunter down the dock. As she sat and pondered the water, I'd kept my desperate gaze on her.

How had she crawled under my skin so fast? She was supposed to be the weird girl from high school. Some crazy chick I had to figure out how to shake. She still laughed the same, but I lived for each moment. She still wore unusual clothing, and this morning I couldn't wait to see what she had on. And to top it all off, she'd paid ten thousand dollars of her own money to charity for her first vacation.

And she refused to talk about herself. Wasn't she supposed to prattle on and be annoying? I had no clue about her. When we'd been younger, she'd asked inane questions about my classes and my sports.

She'd dropped out of school. Had it been that awful for her? Probably. I hadn't enjoyed it and I'd been on the most list—most wanted by the girls, most liked by my classmates, most favored by my teachers.

Then she'd jumped in that damn lake and my heart had stopped.

Even now, my pulse raced when I thought about her disappearing into the vast blue liquid.

But she'd resurfaced when Lynne hadn't.

What the hell had made me open my big mouth and tell Tilly about my sister? No one knew. My lips curled in disgust. My mom certainly never talked about it. She was so angry at Dad about that day as if my old man could have done anything about it.

I sighed and dropped my face into my hands. If I wasn't careful, I'd spill the rest of the story and then Tilly the special-education instructor would think I was worse than shit smeared across her shoe.

"Food's ready," Tilly called, following it up with a shrill laugh.

If she was going to channel Harley Quinn all night, I might self-combust.

Note to self: ask Wes to start pulling *Suicide Squad* comics for me.

"Be right there." I finished up with the tub. It should be ready as soon as we were done eating and cleaning up.

I wolfed through my burger, Tilly's clear joy over her first grilled meal going straight to my cock. Did she know how sexy she sounded, how uninhibited she seemed when she relished something as simple as well-cooked, quality food?

We cleared the table. I was struck by how content I was. Having to work this morning had been, at first, a saving grace. I'd thanked my lucky stars that John Woods was a little too anal for his own good. I'd had to make some calls and double-check details, but the more I'd heard Tilly banging around the cabin, the more restless I'd gotten.

Last weekend, when I was out here to clean the hot tub and check the grill and just do an overall inspection, I'd been thinking about how I just wanted a big project to get lost in, and this cabin wasn't it.

Now, irritation bloomed that John wasn't satisfied with a verbal conversation and emails, that he insisted on meeting with me in person. I would bottle-feed him the data as fast as I could and get back here before Tilly dunked herself again.

I left Tilly to jog upstairs and change into trunks. I'd love to wear absolutely nothing in the hot tub, but that'd only get me where I shouldn't be.

Back downstairs, I couldn't find her in the kitchen. Swearing under my breath, I headed straight for the patio that held the tub.

She was sighing, her arms thrown out to the sides, luxuriating in the swirling water.

That girl didn't wait for anyone.

I slipped in and she didn't move. Either she didn't care, or she hadn't heard me over the jets. I was content to watch her pleasure.

She wiggled and floated her legs up, expressing her delight as freely as she had when eating.

With a long exhale, she opened her eyes and yelped. "When'd you get here?"

I chuckled and eased farther into the water. Heat seeped into my bones, and the long-standing stress that kept my muscles tight oozed out of my fingertips. Never had I relaxed so fully.

"I might just fall asleep," she murmured, her lids drifting shut.

We soaked for a few minutes before she zeroed her gaze back on me. "I'm sorry about earlier."

Dangerous territory. I gave her my most dazzling smile to take her mind off earlier. "Don't worry about it."

She didn't return my grin but seemed to consider me. "I won't go into the lake without telling you again."

I shoved off the bench and floated over next to her. She straightened, brows raised, her gaze sweeping my shoulders and chest. She wasn't going to drop the subject of my reaction to her swimming alone. I'd expected her to be curious. The accident had happened before high school and no one remembered I even had a sister.

Settling next to her, I threw an arm across the back. She scooted a few inches away so she could face me without burying her face in my shoulder, which I wouldn't have minded.

When had cuddling Tilly Johnson become an idea?

"When did it happen?"

She was asking about my sister's accident of course, and she probably assumed Lynne had died. I'd rather let her. My feelings for that nightmarish day sixteen years ago hadn't been resolved and nothing I'd done since then had helped. "Some summer before you changed your name."

She frowned and narrowed her eyes. I could've stayed evasive, but she was just as averse to talking about herself as I was, and I wanted to prove a point.

She licked her bottom lip and looked away. "Before high school then?"

"Yes," I whispered, gazing at her strong profile. The ends of her hair were wet from the water, baring her graceful neck, a neck I wanted to nibble.

But it bothered me. Why had she changed her name? And why wouldn't she tell me? When we were sixteen, I could've snapped my fingers and she would've written a damn book to answer any question I had. Was I losing my appeal?

Anxiety churned in my stomach. After the deliberately atrocious sex, I should be happy. But what if it had worked? What if I had stomped out her crush on me?

Suddenly, knowing the reason behind her name change became the most important thing ever. No—her *telling* me the reason was what counted.

"Who all knows about why you changed your name?"

A moment of panic rippled over her face and she clasped her hands together under the water. "A few people, I guess."

She was getting nervous. Afraid she'd bolt, I edged closer, kept my voice low, steady. "Like your friends now? Or friends from school?"

She cast me a droll look. "There were never any friends from school." Her breath caught, and she tensed.

I turned enough to snake an arm around her and pull her to me. She tilted her head up and I dropped a kiss on her mouth.

"Mara?" I asked.

"What?" She exhaled, her body going molten against mine.

I dropped another kiss along her jawline. "Does Mara know?"

Tilly dropped her head back to give me more access. "No. I haven't known her for very long."

"So it's deeply personal?" I nibbled down her neck, relishing her tiny shiver.

"It's private, yes."

"And you don't talk about private things?" I feathered my hand along her torso, fighting the urge to rip away her swimsuit. But I liked it too much.

"I don't like to talk about it."

I clamped my mouth over a pulse point on her neck and swirled my tongue around it. She squirmed, her legs moving farther apart. I used the move to slide my fingers along the seam of her leg until I reached her sex.

"Flynn…"

I smiled against her skin. "Tell me, Tulip. Why'd you change your name?" Her body went rigid again until I licked a path back up to her mouth. She groaned when I caught her mouth at the same time I dipped under the fabric to spread her folds and circle her nub. I pulled back. "Tulip."

"Don't call me that!" Her flare of frustration rocked her against my hand and her eyelids fluttered. "It…it makes me remember how cruel my dad was."

I jerked back. Not the answer I'd expected. I cursed myself for never having considered she might have such a serious answer.

She gripped my wrist and brought it back. "Can you help me forget?" Her other arm threaded through my hair and shoved my mouth back to hers.

Yes. I'd help her forget. Picking up where I left off, I

massaged her clit. She rode my hand, sending gentle laps of water up to the edge of the hot tub. My erection throbbed, begging for more each time her hip nudged it.

Our tongues twined. I couldn't break the kiss if I tried, she had a ferocious hold on me. She drew her knees up as I tightened my hold on her with my other arm.

Our bodies bumped and she bucked. She wanted more. I moved my hand lower, hitting her clit with my thumb and threading a finger inside.

A low moan escaped us both while we kissed. She was as soft as velvet and burning hot. Her hand was still clamped on my wrist. Thrusting was difficult, but I didn't have to do much. She clutched me and her sex squeezed. How I wanted my cock inside, but I owed her this—for insisting on the story of her name and for leaving her unsatisfied the night before.

I stroked her in sync with my tongue and my hand. Past partners seemed to like that move, but Tilly more than liked it. She writhed like it was my superpower. I totally needed that after my reputation-destroying performance.

She broke our kiss with a gasp, her body arching back. I lined light nips along the cleavage bared by the water.

"Flynn— I— Yes!" Her body went tight with another cry, and my hand flooded with her heat as she shuddered through her orgasm.

I lifted my head to watch my handiwork. Her eyes were squeezed closed, her mouth dropped open, her legs spread wide. Damn, what a fine sight.

She released me and sat up. I mourned the loss of her body heat, even in the steaming water.

"Whoa…that was…that was nice." She laid the back of her hand against her forehead. "Wow, it's really hot in here." Blinking at me like she'd forgotten I was there, her red, kiss-swollen lips formed a timid smile. "Now that was more like it."

"More like what?" Of course. "Oh."

Her eyes flew wide. "Oh. I mean—"

I chuckled. Leave it to Tilly to feel bad for pointing out my failure to pleasure her, though she didn't know I'd set out to do just that. "I know what you mean. About last night—"

"I didn't mean it was bad. It was…"

"Bad." If by bad, I meant losing my load after a few thrusts. "For you."

Her expression was perplexed. "It wasn't bad for you? Oh, shit, I mean—"

"Tilly." At least I wasn't the one stumbling over my words this time. "It looks like I need to prove my sexual prowess." I stood, the water splashing around us, but I stopped. "Um, Tilly, if we do this…"

How could I say it? I'd never had to before. The girls I was with before might hope for more, but they had understood their temporary place in my life.

"I'm not asking for a marriage proposal." She shuddered like it was an awful idea. Shouldn't Crazy J be overly zealous about the prospect? "We both want to have sex. If it's only for this week, so be it. Let's take it one day at a time."

I gawked at the goddess who offered a no-strings-attached week of sex. That meant I wouldn't have to tell her my dark family secret, which meant she wouldn't think I was a worthless asshole, which meant I could fuck Tilly all week long.

I held out my hand and when she clasped it, I yanked her to me. "I might have to pick up another box of condoms."

CHAPTER 7

Tilly

MY BELLY FLUTTERED with delicious nerves. I'd just orgasmed, but my body was already primed for another round. Even if Flynn wasn't any better at sex than our first time, if he could work that kind of magic with his fingers... best vacation ever.

I dried off. We were going to do this. But I doubted he had any protection down here since he was just wearing his swim trunks. Would we make our way upstairs in awkward silence? Would he expect me to say sexy, coquettish things, whatever those would be? As he bent over to dry his legs, an evil idea formed. I wound the towel and snapped him, the fabric cracking in the air just short of his ass.

He snapped straight. "What the—"

With a devilish grin, I used my Harley Quinn imitation. "Race ya!"

Spinning on one foot, I darted for the stairs. The clamber

of Flynn racing through the door spurred my hysterical laughter and I took the stairs two at a time, not caring one bit how much my butt jiggled.

His deep laughter was supremely satisfying. I streaked down the hall, about to go to my room, but he likely had the condoms in his, so I veered into his bedroom and dove onto the bed.

Bouncing, I was still laughing when he landed on top of me on his hands and knees. His grin was stretched wide and he was breathing hard from the quick sprint. His impressive erection caught my attention. Broad from tip to base, he was hard and straining for me. I'd wanted more of it last night and I'd make sure that happened tonight.

"When'd you take your trunks off?"

His green eyes gleamed with intent. "That was the reason I didn't catch you."

"I'm getting your bedding wet."

"You will be," he growled, sending a wave of heat through my core. He wove his fingers through my straps and dragged them down, staring at my breasts when they bounced free.

My nipples were painfully erect and when he lowered his head and dragged his tongue across one, I whimpered. "More."

He seemed to forget about my swimsuit as he tongued my nipples, first one, then the other. I cradled his head, shivering at the air wafting over my wet skin and the fiery sensations he was sending through my body. I arched my back. He released my nipple with a pop to peel the rest of my suit off. Tossing it aside, he dropped his body down, his lips on my stomach.

I was giddy with excitement. So...no *wham, bam* tonight— I was getting the royal treatment.

He kissed and licked his way down to the apex of my thighs. "Flynn?"

He raised his head enough to cock an eyebrow.

How did I even… I didn't want to dissuade him, but if he failed again, I wanted him to know it wasn't his fault. "I just got off."

"Yeah?"

"Say I do it again while you're…down there. Then I probably won't when we…"

His smile sent a wave of lust through me. He wedged himself between my legs, my knees up, feet on his shoulders. "Tilly, baby, let me show you what I can really do."

His hot mouth cupped my nub and his tongue attacked me. I wrenched off the bed with a gasp of ecstasy. That felt *good*. He worked me until I was needy, rocking against him for more, before he inserted first one finger, then two. Only, the intrusion was slow and steady, unlike his tongue on my clit. The dichotomy was too much for my nerves. I wanted to be filled with him, but for the love of all things sexual, I didn't want him to ease up with his tongue. A second orgasm was imminent. Sure, that'd happened before—when I'd done it myself after a date that'd ended in mediocre sex, and it had been mostly to see if it could actually happen.

He set a steady, slow rhythm with his fingers. Then he tilted his head and *oooh*… Was he sucking on my clit?

With little warning, I exploded. I would've jackknifed off the bed, but he held me in place until I fell limp. He could impale me and go about his business and I didn't care to move a muscle, but I'd miss being an active participant.

He reared over me, his gaze intense, his chin glistening from my juices, but he didn't rush to don the condom, hadn't even pulled out the box.

"What you're saying is," he planted his hands on either side of my body, "that you've never had three orgasms in one night before."

"Truth. Have you?"

He lifted a shoulder. "Eh, maybe."

Not the response I expected. "How could you not remember? Did you have more?" I sounded shrill. I snapped my mouth shut. When I got shrill, Flynn started to stutter.

But this time, all he did was lift the side of his mouth. "I guess if I did, they weren't worth remembering."

She nodded. "I get that. An empty orgasm."

His gaze stuck on mine. "Yeah. Empty."

A girl could take those words the wrong way. Like I'd be an empty orgasm for him, too. But the stark realization in his gaze chased those thoughts away.

My body was recovering from round two, but my goal wasn't to get myself off. I wrapped my arms and legs around Flynn and pulled him down to me, seeking some way to deepen the connection between us. I'd wanted Flynn forever, but that was with the fervor of a young girl who'd made her crush out to be everything she'd needed him to be at the time. Today, he was just Flynn, a man who needed his bed partner to care about him. And I did, even if I couldn't share all of me with him. We weren't the same kids we used to be, but Flynn would always be special to me.

Our mouths met for a languid kiss, his erection pressed between us. He shifted until he stroked my wet folds. One little tweak and he'd be at my entrance. He broke our kiss to nip along my neck as he reached for the nightstand. While he took care of the condom, I ran my hands over his broad shoulders. A few scars marred his hands and wrists.

He noticed me tracing them with my fingers. "Hazards of the trade when you don't do things right the first time."

I loosened my legs to give him room to roll the condom on. "I like them. The rest of you is…"

He paused. "Is what?"

"Too perfect."

His gaze swept my body where it held his. I was spread

under him, completely naked and more open than I'd ever been with a guy, but I wasn't embarrassed. No negative emotions were allowed to rain on my time with him. But there was no denying which of us ate right and got a lot of physical activity in this bed. Defined abs, firm pecs, and solid legs. He was nothing but muscle.

"See. Your body's sick."

The corners of his mouth kicked up. "And you were holding out on me with yours."

"What do you mean?"

"I'll show you."

He placed himself and my breath caught. *Don't let me down.* I couldn't ignore that I'd fantasized about how Flynn would shame all my former lovers.

He didn't shove in and get down to business, he fed himself inside of me, so slowly I almost started begging.

Rolling my hips up, my voice came out whiny. "Flynn."

He jerked forward and impaled me. I closed my eyes and sighed. The only thing that had kept our first time together from sucking was how well he'd filled me. Just being seated within me, he hit so many of the right places.

The air rushed out of him and he collapsed to his forearms. "Tilly."

Wrapping my legs back around him, I twined my arms around his neck. He slid out, then crashed back in, his ass clenching under my calves.

A whimper escaped. Shouldn't I be too sensitive or too numb for it to feel this good already?

Another lingering slide out, then he swiveled his hips and teased his way in.

His forehead touched mine. "Tilly, you're killing me. It's all I can do to hold back."

"Don't then." *Just fuck me!*

"No, I need to prove myself." Another leisurely thrust,

belied by all the desperate tension in his body. He set an unhurried pace, goading me into desperation.

"I think you've proved yourself enough. I need more."

A low chuckle vibrated through his chest into mine. "I told you to let me show you what I can do."

He claimed my mouth again as he claimed my body. His shaft stroked my desire to violent flames until I was panting at the effort of keeping up with him. A third climax built, and he hadn't even had one.

He'd proved himself, so thoroughly.

Then what had last night been?

Before the question could burrow in, he wedged a hand between us. His finger landed on my clit. I twitched. Too much, that was too much!

But he just rested his hand there as he rode me, his tongue licking me senseless and his hips plunging into me over and over again.

I squeezed my legs and wrenched back, but his other arm was a steel band that anchored me to him.

The orgasm crested and I cried and moaned, but he didn't ease up. I shook, my legs clamping down hard, then falling loose as I rode out the massive wave of ecstasy. My core was coiled so tight I feared I'd create a void within, then fly apart, only to collapse in on myself again. Over and over until I was dizzy with the release.

Flynn grunted and slammed into me one last time, his entire body an unyielding wall of man on top of me. He shuddered and groaned, but maintained contact, his kiss morphing from urgent to languid as his climax faded. He held my clit hostage with nothing but the pressure of his finger, but he released it and wrapped his arm around me.

I was breathing like I'd run a 5K. His chest heaved as if this round had been as profound for him as it had for me. Because Flynn had blown every freaking guy off the planet.

He looked as good as he did *and* he could conjure an orgasm from me as deftly as Dr. Strange summoned a new realm.

Best vacation ever.

∼

Flynn

I WOKE to a warm body curved into me. Tilly slept as freely as she lived life, sprawled half across me and over the rest of the bed. Her mouth was slightly open as she puffed air, a thick chunk of light brown hair plastered over her face.

Damn, she was cute.

Despite the sun shining through the picture window and the birds chirping cheerful melodies outside, a cloud dimmed my outlook on the day. I had to run to town and meet with John Woods. Normally after spending the night with a girl, I was planning two things: one last round or two of sex, and a good excuse to get the fuck out of Dodge. A work meeting was hands-down the best, but I didn't want to leave the bed.

I should get a quick run and a workout in before I left. The sheets were tenting admirably, thanks to the sex bunny I'd uncovered in Tilly. So a good workout and cold shower were even more warranted to keep me from sprouting another erection during my meeting.

An unbidden smile appeared on my face. Tilly had surprised both of us. She'd been an uninhibited and enthusiastic partner. No shyness, no hiding her body. She accepted herself. And she should. Curves in all the right places, she was so free with herself and me that she had the most astounding orgasms until I thought she'd clamp off all blood supply to my dick. And she didn't do it on purpose. No artful body positioning, no whatever the hell those vaginal calisthenics women did to fake enjoyment. Just Tilly coming like a force of nature. I was one lucky son of a bitch to have experienced it—to have been the one to cause it.

As if my ego in the bedroom needed more stroking, but once puberty had passed, sex was just one more thing I'd had to master and dominate. And last night, I'd dominated.

Carefully, I extracted myself from my slumbering partner. *Fucking work.*

I sat up and shook my head. I never thought like that. It was always *fucking time off.*

Dressing in running shorts and a T-shirt, I made little noise, but Tilly rolled over, letting out a soft moan in her sleep. Her head popped up with a floof of hair. She rolled again to face me.

"Morning." She yawned and pushed her hair out of her face. I wanted to fist my hand in that hair and take her again.

I'd gotten a pack of twelve condoms, but I'd need to pick another one up if we were going to share a bed this week.

"Hey. I'm going for a quick run before I leave for the city."

She stretched her hands overhead and fuuuck... Her breasts jutted up to the ceiling, her lean legs curved at an enticing angle. A quickie instead of a run would— No. Too soon for my pride for a quickie. And since we'd had another round in the middle of the night, she could use a recharge.

"I should try a run. Is there a nice trail nearby, or should I run on the road?"

I should offer to go with her, but I hated missing my workout. I kept my runs short and hard because I usually had a long day of work in front of me.

She must've noticed my indecision. "Don't wait for me." Waving me off, she sat all the way up. "I have all day to bond with nature."

Guilt ate at me. What had made me think sneaking away for a day of work was okay?

I didn't dare touch her before I left. "I'll have my phone on me if you need anything," I called as I walked out of the room.

" 'Kay." Her soft footsteps faded as she went into her bedroom to dress.

I frowned as I went down the stairs. If she was okay with me leaving for the day, then I shouldn't whine about it.

My run wasn't as brutal as usual. I let up on my pace and stuck to the dirt roads that wound around the lake and its various cabins. Vibrant green trees surrounded me, rustling in the breeze. Glittering blue beckoned. The water would be nice. Tilly wanted to go fishing. I hadn't been fishing in forever, always had too much to do, and lacked the gumption to sit on a boat with nothing but my thoughts. But with Tilly… I'd have to rent a boat in town, but I'd make it happen. I looked forward to it.

After a couple of miles, I turned around and sped up. If I dithered any longer, I'd be late and John was already antsy about the project. He was only my age and I suspected that was why he was so skittish about trusting such a big project to me. But I had come highly recommended, and even I could tell the dude was all about image.

The cabin came into sight and so did the swaying, scrumptious behind of Tilly. I started covering the distance between us. Startled, she whipped around to look at me—and skidded over a loose patch of gravel. My chest froze as she went down, sprawled on the ground. That had to have done some damage.

"Oh, shit." I sprinted the rest of the way, but she was already on her feet, brushing herself off.

"I'm so clumsy." She threw me a smile and started jogging.

I fell in next to her and peeked down at her knee. "You're bleeding."

"Just a little road rash. Wow, it's so gorgeous out here."

Her breathy tone reminded me of sex, but I glanced back down to her knee. She hit a good pace, one I honestly hadn't expected of her, but a rivulet of blood ran down her leg. I'd gotten enough road rash to know how painful it was, but she'd barely paused.

"Do you want to stop and take care of your wound?" I wanted to stop and take care of her wound.

"Nah. We don't have anything for it here anyway. It'll wash off in the shower and I'll slap a bandage on it." She passed me a smile when she caught my perplexed stare. "Really, it's okay. I'm a big girl."

With a high pain tolerance. I'd been known to limp home after a wipeout. We were a few hundred yards from the cabin when she punched me on the shoulder.

"Race ya!" She sped off.

I could only shake my head before I raced after her. I passed her—sort of—easily and reached the cabin first.

I stopped to stretch, but she darted up the porch and ran inside, her laughter filtering out. "I'm going to shower," she yelled from inside. "Wanna conserve water?"

I'd been about to drop for some pushups, but the inner debate over whether to finish my workout or fuck a hot chick in the shower was over in a heartbeat. Rushing in the cabin and up the stairs, I was about to detour for a condom when I spied a trail of foil packets leading to the guest bathroom.

When had she…

I didn't care. Snagging one on my way, I was naked before I hit the bathroom.

CHAPTER 8

illy

"I THINK we should go out to eat tonight," Flynn said.

I dipped my fishing rod, hoping to entice a bite. No luck. "Sure."

The fishing boat rocked with the waves. We were in the middle of the lake, and instead of nervous tendrils twisting my gut, I was as relaxed as I'd ever been. I still didn't know how to swim, but Flynn had bought me a life jacket and refused to let me pay him back. It was already Saturday and he'd been treating me to my bucket-list vacation all week.

Stellar sex—a few times a day. Hiking, done. Fishing, done. Fishing out of a boat—I hadn't caught a damn thing but done. Swimming in the lake. Flynn had worked with me on some swimming strokes, then given up, but he was determined to teach me something. He'd made me promise to take lessons when I returned home. I'd only accepted because now I wouldn't be saving every penny for the adult resource center.

"I don't think they're biting today. Let's head back." Flynn packed up. He fished and maneuvered the boat like he came out here every weekend.

Maybe he did. After almost a whole week together, I still didn't know much about him. But I knew him. He was a perfectionist, for some reason I hadn't figured out yet. If he found any tiny task to be done in the cabin, he was on it. That giant truck of his carried a massive toolbox in the back. I loved watching him tinker. The subtle tension in his face eased as he lost himself in the task. He liked to take care of himself, but I'd noticed more carbs sneaking onto his plate and he was no longer killing himself with every morning workout. He'd even worn athletic shorts and a performance T all day yesterday instead of his usual jean shorts and polo.

His job must be stressful for him to have so visibly relaxed since arriving a week ago. When I'd first seen him at Arcadia, he'd worn his suit like a second skin—or so it had seemed at the time. But I bet if I crossed paths with him again, Flynn would be pulling at his collar or twitching his cuffs like he couldn't wait to shed his apparel.

When we retired to the cabin in the evenings, we didn't just go to bed, nor did we each talk about ourselves. Instead, we had Iron Man and Captain America marathons. I'd even produced *Suicide Squad* and he'd requested that I put the swimsuit on again so he could rip it off—with his teeth.

My Puddin'.

We reached the dock and he helped me off. I took care of the tackle while he got the boat hooked to the pickup. Tomorrow we'd go back to regular life, so he had to return the boat tonight.

I couldn't fight the heavy feeling of this week coming to an end. My resolve to keep everyone at a distance was fading around Flynn. My mission to pay back my debts had been accomplished. Well, except for my school loans, but those just cut into my fun money more than anything.

It was daunting to think about talking about my life with someone. After the hot tub incident, I'd been prepared for Flynn to ask. Only he hadn't.

Disappointment sat like lead in my belly. Like me, he seemed to be making the most of our time together but not digging too deep so we could part ways.

Did I want to go back to a Flynn-less life?

What about him? He didn't seem worse for wear after spending a week with Crazy J. Other than being more relaxed, he laughed more every day we were together. Each superhero movie we watched spurred conversations about what we'd played with as kids. It was a safe topic and we didn't venture beyond our experiences with the toys.

I'd tried to learn his favorites. Work. Candy? He didn't eat candy. I'd die without Hot Tamales. Color? Whatever he stripped off me. I couldn't pick just one color. Pet? I'd said cat and changed the subject.

After everything was put away, I went into the cabin and up to my room. Well, his room. My stuff had migrated over by Tuesday, when it had become apparent we were tearing through the stash of condoms.

I dug through my clothes to find something suitable for eating out. Flynn's footsteps landed behind me and a smile twitched my lips. He liked me bent over, and I liked that he liked it.

I straightened with an armload of clothing. "What kind of place are we going to? I need to know what to wear."

He kissed my neck and I leaned into him. "Wear whatever."

Eying my linen shorts and plain shirts, I was grateful I'd packed something without an emblem of some kind.

Standing out in a crowd was my thing, but with Flynn, I didn't want to be Crazy J.

He backed up and I missed his heat. With a light touch, he spun me around. "What's wrong?"

I looked into his green depths, eyes I loved gazing into, then back down at my plain-as-hell clothing. "I don't know what to wear."

He chuckled. "There's nothing fancy—it's a lake resort town. There'll be pizza places and bars and grills. We'll go someplace fun to celebrate our last night here."

"Okay." The faint churning in my belly was back. Last night with Flynn. Did it bother him, too?

The cabin was his, though. He could come back anytime he wanted...with anyone he wanted. I worried my lower lip. Wow. That thought fed the acid boiling in my stomach.

"Tilly, what's wrong?"

He stood in front of me like a wall and his voice was full of concern—for me. How long had I wanted someone to care about me? And Flynn genuinely seemed to. When I went back home and spent my nights alone, at least I'd have that.

I answered with honesty, but not full disclosure. "I'm sad my vacation's coming to an end."

His eyes dimmed. "Yeah, me too. I needed it."

"Maybe we can do it again sometime." My tone was light, joking, but the words fell hard between us.

"Maybe." We said nothing for a moment and I shifted my feet. He wasn't looking for a wife and I wasn't looking for a husband, but the silence made me feel like I'd asked for a life-time commitment.

He dug in my bundle of clothing and withdrew a gauzy blue top. "Wear this. It brings out your eyes." He tossed it on the bed, went back to my clothing, and snagged a pair of white shorts. "And this because they make your legs look a mile long and I want to peel them off you."

I giggled as I shoved the rest of my armload in the suitcase. "That's, like, the plainest outfit I've ever worn. If I see one of my students, it'll be like I'm Clark Kent with the glasses. They won't recognize me. They'd be so disappointed if they saw me this week."

An odd expression swept through his features. "You dress up for them?"

I shrugged. "It's fun."

"What was your excuse in high school?" His question sounded like a joke, but all humor drained from me.

I snapped the shorts from his hands. "I wore what I had available."

Stepping around him, I went to the bed and picked up my shirt. Wacky clothes plus jaw wired shut plus social awkwardness equaled Crazy J. I refused to apologize for being myself. And Flynn—

"Tilly, I was kidding."

I spun, holding my shirt and shorts close to my chest. A part of me argued to keep my mouth shut, but I never listened, not even when it'd earned me a broken jaw. "You were. But here's the thing. I'm still Crazy J." I'd started to hate that name almost as much as Tulip. "I can't change how I dressed then, or how I acted, and since I'm standing here, a survivor of my childhood, I don't want to." Stop talking! "I liked you a lot, that was no secret. But you were one of the few guys I never caught laughing at me. You even helped when the mean girls ganged up. You seemed to not mind how I was. So I'm a little hurt to find out that I was a freak to you, too."

He stared at me for a second. "What exactly happened when you were a kid?"

"I don't want to talk—"

"I know, but you've told me enough that I can deduce

89

what went on." He folded his arms and sat on the edge of the bed. "I'd like to hear it from you."

"Why? After tomorrow, are we going to talk again?" My frustrations from the week welled and I let them roll off my tongue. "Are we going to hook up or are you going to take me out?" I laughed and brushed a strand of hair behind my ear, his gaze tracking the move. "I can see it now. You in your suit and expensive truck, taking me out after Wacky Monday at school."

"Wacky Monday?" Understanding dawned and he nodded. "That was why you were—"

"And the rest of the week isn't much better. The kids love it and I do, too. I quit caring about what people thought of me when it was obvious they didn't care about me in the first place. Unless I have some pretentious bitch as a client who won't pay me unless I dress to the lowest of her standards, then I dress how I want and fuck what others think."

"That's freedom not all of us have," he muttered. I was about to ask him what he meant when he kept going, his voice low. "Why'd you drop out of school, Tilly? Why'd you change your name? Why did you bid such a specific amount?"

I stomped to my luggage and dropped my items on top. Going out for dinner was no longer appealing. Tears burned the backs of my eyes because the thing was, I wanted to tell him. I wanted him to care about me, but he didn't. He was only asking for the story, and I had no idea why.

If I let my past spill out, maybe I could just pretend that Flynn cared, that the emotions I unleashed wouldn't scare him off. If they did, then he wasn't the guy for me. An easy platitude, but after the last week with him, I couldn't imagine another man in my life. "My dad was abusive and my mom was passive and afraid of losing him. When he'd rage, she wouldn't step in. After each episode, her depression got worse until she quit buying groceries, quit buying food. Clothes shopping? Forget it. I pilfered money from both of them and when I got caught…" I paused to gulp because I'd never admitted this to anyone. "Well, I might've talked funny with my jaw wired shut, but it was harder to talk with a broken jaw."

Color leeched from Flynn's face, but I continued. "I should've left home after that, but Mom stepped in to care for me. I like to think she felt guilty, but she'd never admit it. Why'd I drop out? I left home after Dad caught me feeding a stray cat our precious milk that he'd bought from a gas station because Mom never picked any up."

My throat swelled and I blinked rapidly, but the tears rolled down my cheek.

"He beat the cat, then he started on me."

I sniffled and looked around for a tissue. There were none.

"But I got away." I swiped at my eyes. "Why the specific amount? That's how much of my hospital bill the Center for Abuse Recovery covered. I didn't even count the supplies and food they gave me while I stayed there. Or the support I got to get my GED. I owe them more than I can ever pay, but it was the least I could do."

Flynn stayed quiet, his expression grim.

I lifted a shoulder. "So that's my shitty life story. I've never told anyone. I have no relationship with my parents and my life is my work. So, that's me. What about you?"

≈

Flynn

.   .   .

I NEEDED A DRINK, but I couldn't do anything that'd take me away from Tilly. "I can't believe you went through all that. How did I not know?"

She rolled her eyes at me.

Yeah, I deserved that look. I'd thought of her as nothing more than Crazy J, had wanted her to walk away and leave me in peace. Asking about her life hadn't occurred to me then, and I'd been avoiding asking the past week. Tilly was a drug. I wanted more and more and more until her absence would leave me shaking with need. Work on Monday would've been hard enough after the week with Tilly, but I would've pushed through, trying to forget her.

As if I could ever forget her.

I patted the spot next to me, staring her down until she trudged to the bed and plopped beside me.

"I'm sorry." When was the last time I'd apologized to anyone? It certainly wasn't because I was perfect. In my business, admitting I'd done something wrong threatened my future. I worked tirelessly to make sure I didn't have to apologize. And as for personal relationships... I didn't see Wes and Mara enough. "I'm sorry I didn't know everything you've been through."

"No one does," she said quietly. "Only my parents know. I'm sure in their story, I'm the villain."

"You were a kid!" I knew the feeling all too well. In my mom's eyes, I'd morphed into the villain over time. Everything was my fault in the story of Mom.

"No." She twisted her hands in her lap. "I never had the chance to be a kid."

"Is that why you work with them? Children?"

"Probably. I love their innocence and their energy and the challenge of working to get through to them, finding the way they each learn best." A slow smile spread across her face and she turned to prop a knee beside me. "I started my own tutoring business, and someday, I want to expand my business, like get a building, have some staff." Her grin broadened and she spread her hands wide. "A place specializing in alternative learning. I've been coming up with ways to raise funds, find sponsors, and offer scholarships. Sadly, the lessons cost a family a fortune. Worth every penny, but it's hard to find the pennies, even when they know how much it'd benefit their kid."

"You're unreal." In so many ways. How far out of my league could she get? In my career, I wanted to build the finest product I could, and my products happened to be businesses. I'd aspired to get in with the movers and shakers of the city, the ones with enough power, money, and influence to build banks, office plazas, and strip malls. Once Flynn Halstengard was the go-to name for high-end construction, the guy to pay top dollar for, I might finally be able to distance myself from Flynn Halstengard, the kid who let his sister almost drown and failed to help his mom.

Tilly playfully shoved at my chest. "You make me sound like I'm a superhero. I just want to give back to the world, to be that person who's there when someone needs me."

And I'd been raised by a woman who had no clue what that meant. My mom thought everyone had failed her. Dad. Me. Abe, for not offering her monetary support. Her coworkers, for not understanding that she should be able to miss three weeks of work because life "got to be too much." Too much of what? It certainly hadn't been taking care of her children. I would've starved if Abe hadn't taken me in.

But what was I complaining about? Tilly had lived a nightmare. And had still turned out better than me.

"After tonight…" She was back to twisting her hands together. "What about us?"

I let out a slow exhale. What about us? All I'd prepared for was a week at the lake. If the lady who purchased me wanted sex and I was willing, even better. But "a thing" hadn't been in my plans. A thing with Crazy J had never occurred to me.

I grasped her hand, a blush of melancholy staining my mood. "I'm not going to lie. My job doesn't leave much room for fun. I'm going to be swamped catching up after this week." She tried to hide her disappointment, but it was in her eyes. And she was awful at hiding her emotions. "I don't want to force anything. Can I give you a call?"

The question soured in my mouth. How many times had I used that line? *I'll call you.* But if there was one way to redeem myself, it was to not string her along, not give her hope that I wanted something long-term.

She glanced down at our clasped hands, a tiny furrow developing between her brows. "Thank you for being honest."

"It's the least I can do. For what it's worth, I'm glad you won the bid." The curdled taste in my mouth seeped down to flip my stomach. I'd almost gotten in my own way of having a fabulous weekend. My gut eased with relief that Tilly had won me and that she hadn't been hurt further by my attempt to manipulate the bidding. "I need to take you out to eat."

She squeezed my hand, then jumped up. Stripping her clothes off, she wiggled into the outfit I'd picked out.

I groaned and she shot me a wicked look. "Not until after supper, Puddin'."

That name. Got me every time.

"I thought spilling my guts would wipe out my appetite, but nope." She leaned over and kicked a hip out, giving me a full view of her cleavage. "I'm starving."

I looked my fill of her soft flesh. "Then you need to get to my truck first. Because if I catch you, we're not gonna make it to the restaurant."

She squealed and took off, her fantastic ass flexing under

her shorts and rushing more blood to my cock, as if that weren't where it was headed anyway.

Giving her a head start suited my purpose. She wanted to go out and what Tilly wanted, I'd give her. And the sooner we got to the restaurant and got distracted, the sooner she'd forget I still hadn't answered her question.

CHAPTER 9

illy

I PARKED AT THE WOODS' obnoxious home and checked my phone for the twentieth time that day.

No messages.

No missed calls.

On the bright side, I wouldn't be going into a tutoring session out of my mind with excitement that Flynn had called.

I'd spilled my history to him. And he hadn't wanted much to do with me after. A dam of hope had burst open inside of me when I'd laid it all out. We'd gone out for supper and back to the cabin for hot, needy sex for hours. Then woken up to have goodbye sex. At the time, I'd told myself it wasn't goodbye sex. After what we'd gone through, he'd want to see me again.

Totally.

But two weeks had gone by. I was deep into my summer schedule with no social calendar.

Maybe I ought to get one.

I blew the hair out of my eyes. Yeah, and I hadn't the first clue how to do that.

One more look.

Nothing. I wiped all thoughts of Flynn and sex from my mind. If I didn't do it now, it'd happen when Mrs. Woods greeted me with a pained smile and found a reason to belittle me for something.

Each time I encountered the woman, a spark of bitterness flared that I had to depend on someone like her for money. Each time, I quashed it and ran through the multitude of good things that had come my way, especially the clients who weren't condescending hags.

I scrambled out of the car and rushed to the entrance.

Berta opened seconds after the first ring of the doorbell. The older woman emanated exhaustion and her shoulders hung in defeat. "Uffda, Tilly. It's been a helluva day."

I stepped inside. "Are you almost done? I see a long, warm soak in your future."

Berta huffed. "I don't think my bath salts can wash away Charlie's screaming."

"Another bad day for him?" I fortified myself. He'd been having more off days these last few weeks than normal. Well, his normal. "They're going to need to pad his room if he keeps up his tantrums."

Last Monday, he'd busted his forehead open. I'd gotten zero teaching in, spending most of my time coaxing him into allowing me to put on a bandage to stop the trickle of blood. It might've needed stitches or those bandage strips, but Mrs. Woods hadn't been interested. *Are you telling me he got hurt again on your watch?*

97

As if she hadn't known he'd smacked his forehead against the edge of the desk. It'd happened before I had arrived.

I scurried into Charlie's custom learning room. He was self-soothing in the corner.

"Hey, Charlie." He continued rocking, his little hands manipulating a texture cube. It was one of his favorite soothers, with different materials on each side.

I folded down next to him, speaking softly. He wouldn't look at me, but after several minutes, his brown gaze finally darted in my direction.

Score.

I worked diligently with him for our hour together, my concern growing. A subdued Charlie worried me. Could it be something as simple as a growth spurt that was wearing him out and decreasing his tolerance for the world around him?

Our time was wrapping up when the door flung open.

"Charlie buddy." Mr. Woods strode in, his tweed suit jacket hanging open and his tie undone. But his ultra-bleached white smile was on me and not his son.

I was only happy to see him for one reason: I wouldn't have to track down Mrs. Woods and update her on Charlie's progress. "Charlie and I just finished. Can I chat with you about our hour before I go?"

I had to be brutally specific with my request. Otherwise, he would lead me to his office to "talk." Or back me into a wall as he "listened closely."

His gaze traveled down to my sedate sandals and back up my legs. Dammit, why hadn't I worn capris at the very least?

Oh, right. Because I shouldn't have to.

"Sure, Tilly. Let me hug the big guy first."

Not for the first time, I hoped Mr. Woods was serious about his enthusiasm in greeting his son and not using it as a way to get into my plain khaki bottoms.

He squatted by Charlie and pulled him in for a hug. A piercing shriek rang out and Charlie pushed his dad away, scurrying back to his soothing corner.

A frown pulled at my lips. For all his faults, Mr. Woods was one of Charlie's favorite people.

"That's what I wanted to talk to you about," I said my goodbyes to Charlie, grabbed my tote, and crept out the door.

Mr. Woods was on my heels. I spun and faced his chest.

"Oh." Taking a step back and clutching my bag in front of me to give myself as much personal space as possible, I filled him in on my observations of Charlie's behavior. "So, I have no idea what's going on, but I'm still making progress as far as teaching him shapes and colors. He's learning."

"Great. Yeah. Is the nanny coming tonight?"

"I don't know. You'll have to ask Mrs. Woods." I'd be surprised if the nanny was coming. The turnover rate was high. I assumed it was for two reasons: they got tired of Mr. Woods's advances, or Mrs. Woods sniffed out the too-close working relationship.

His voice dropped an octave and he tilted his head to give me a smirk. His artfully coiffed hair was probably designed for the move. "Aren't you going to stay until she does?"

"I'm sorry, but I have another client after this." I sidled around him. "Have a good night."

"See you next week, Tilly." He made it sound like a promise.

I shuddered. That man was an egocentric, selfish, rich dick who was too used to people jumping through his hoops. Only an hour a week I had to deal with him. He had no more control over my life than that.

∾

Flynn

I SAT BACK in my desk chair and propped my feet on the glass top, Bluetooth in my ear. My cleaning crew would curse me later. The other half of the desk was a standing workstation and I had a ball chair pushed in the corner. But it was the end of a long day after an especially rough week, and I wanted to lounge for the few minutes I'd been able to all week.

I pinched the bridge of my nose. A tension headache throbbed at my temples.

I'd done nothing to relieve stress since I'd come home from vacation to a pile of emails that'd taken me days to comb through.

A prospective client wanted my company to draw up plans for a luxurious retail and office complex. One of my current projects had hit a delay with the concrete that could've pushed the project behind a month if I hadn't fast-talked any and every contractor in the city that provided cement. And then there was John Woods, who jabbered on the other end of my earbud.

"We'll need to reschedule Monday's meeting," Woods said. "I have to bang my nanny. It's her last day and I never know if the missus is going to hire a fatty or not."

What a dick.

I stared at my computer monitor, tapped a few buttons, and pulled up my schedule. When it came to those writing the checks, I scheduled meetings in person. My assistant, Matthew, was awesome, but it gave the moguls the warm fuzzies to feel like I was at their beck and call. And I sort of was. "No problem. Tuesday?" Please, not Tuesday. My day was packed with meetings and I wanted to sneak in job site visits in my off-hours.

"Damn. My day is crazy. Let's talk over drinks. Seven?"

My eyelids slid shut. Cocktails with Woods was the last thing I wanted to do with my Tuesday evening. Any evening. The guy commented on the boobs of every female who walked by. I constantly rode the line of humoring the man and trying to ignore the perverted remarks, deciding on the minimum I could say so I didn't antagonize a top client, yet not sell my soul downriver for money.

I confirmed the time and got my client off the phone.

Matthew watched me, iPad prepped and ready for the instructions I had been in the middle of before Woods's call.

"Change the Woods meeting on Monday to seven Tuesday at the usual place for drinks."

"Ugh, I hate that place," Matthew muttered, clicking through the instructions. "It's like a pretentious watering hole for egotistical giraffes that need to neck-whack each other into thinking they're glorious, elegant creatures."

I snorted. "That's so damn accurate. We all have our vices, I guess."

"And Mr. Woods's is boobs and nannies. I'm tempted to tell Bryant to pull him over one day, give him a ticket, and make his community service to quit being a shitty husband."

Matthew's candor in private was half the reason I kept him around. If we didn't have a professional relationship to maintain, we could be friends. "Do it, just not until after we're done with his bank."

"I hope I don't have to give you a big ole 'I told you so' over Mr. Woods. He's trouble."

"He's an asshole with money who can build a bank. I don't discriminate." I listed what I'd need Matthew to do next week and shooed him out for the weekend.

Sighing, I rubbed my face and checked the time. Eight o'clock on a Friday night. The sun was still out and the clubs were probably coming alive.

I should go out.

Taking my Bluetooth out, I flung it on the desk. I stared at the floor, then dug out my phone and texted Wes.

Whatcha doing tonight?

It was a long shot, but maybe Wes would be free and we could hang. The first weekend home from the lake, I'd spent all night on the floor of Wes's rec room, getting my ass kicked by Mara. She had the new Zelda game for the Switch and had schooled me. I'd almost skipped it, knowing Tilly questions were inevitable.

All I'd said was that she wasn't what I'd expected and I'd spent the week doing whatever she wanted, like fishing and hiking. Not a lie. All the sex we'd had was between me and Tilly.

Mara's jaw drop had almost been insulting. I'd spent the rest of the evening avoiding Wes's pointed looks and managed not to answer any more questions about Tilly.

The second weekend, I'd found the water line to my fridge leaking. The drywall behind the fridge was soft and warped and I'd spent the weekend replacing and repainting it. My kitchen might not have needed a repaint, but it'd gotten one. Since I'd been at it and all.

And now I'd arrived at my third weekend by myself. My old routine of finding bedmates for each night held no appeal, but my body constantly reminded me that I missed sex. I missed curves, Harley Quinn bikinis, a breathy laugh, a needy sigh, the way Tilly arched back into…

Not helping. I should just go home and go to bed since I planned on rising early to work out and check job sites.

My phone *pinged*. *At the new Wonder Woman movie.*

The new one was out? I could go watch a sexy Amazon kick ass in a leotard.

By myself?

No deal. But Wes was with Mara. My friend would probably go again if I asked, but I didn't feel like being a charity case.

I drummed my fingers on the desktop. The image of Tilly clutching her Wonder Woman bag flitted through my mind.

Before I could tell myself what a bad idea it was, I had Tilly's number pulled up and hit dial.

There was no going back.

It rang. And rang.

Shit. Who'd been a dumbass and assumed she'd be perched by her phone, waiting on me?

This guy.

Her voicemail kicked on and I froze. Her cheerful voice telling me to leave a message yanked my heartstrings. Now that I was settled back into my daily grind, just listening to her highlighted the dullness in my life.

Disconnecting, I stared at my office. It was chic. Modern. Contemporary. It also lacked color with its glass desk and its black streamlined furniture that made the gray in the carpet pop. Well, there was the blue sky in the pictures of all my past projects mounted on my wall, my version of the "I love me" wall. Ironically, Arcadia added the most color to my environment, with its vibrant marquis. The multifaceted display drew eyes for miles.

Arcadia was my pride and joy, and since I'd moved on from building houses, it had also been my simplest project.

And Mara and her partner, Chris, had been easier to deal with than John Woods.

My phone vibrated and I almost dropped it. Flustered I said "answer" but my Bluetooth was lying on my desk. Tilly's name flashed on the screen, along with a picture I'd taken of her standing at the water's edge with her back to me, the Batman insignia on the ass of her bikini a stark contrast to the natural environment. I'd shown her the picture and she'd laughed and pointed out how odd she looked surrounded by sparkling blue water and lush trees, wearing a Dark Knight suit.

I missed that laugh.

Fumbling with my phone, I finally got it answered. "Hey."

"Hi," she whispered on the other end. "Sorry I missed your call. I'm at the movies and wasn't going to answer."

Her, too? "Are you with Wes and Mara?" If my friends were all out without me, and I was sitting in my office on a Friday night, I deserved to wear this stupid suit for another three hours.

"They're here? I didn't see them walk in. Maybe they're at another theater. Wanna come over?"

"You-You're not with anyone?"

"I don't know anyone who'd sit through the same movie three times with me. This is my second time. I plan to get in on the 10:15 showing, too. Oh, shit, the previews are starting, I gotta go. There's a seat still open by me. Want me to save it?"

"Yes."

She hung up and I was out of my office in seconds.

Striding to my pickup, I shrugged out of my suit coat and yanked off my tie. I undid my cuffs and rolled them. I had clean gym clothes in my office but didn't want to take the time to change into them. The movie was starting and a seat was being saved for me.

illy

My heart leaped into my throat as I watched the shadowy figure jog up the stairs. I always sat in the middle of the back row, but no one had ever looked like Flynn on the theater stairs.

His hair was perfectly styled, like a blond Tony Stark. Maybe it was the suit. He'd lost the jacket, opened the first button, and rolled his sleeves up, but that didn't detract from the fit. Like how his slacks hugged his trim waist but gave his ass and thighs enough room to flex underneath. And the bulge of his biceps... The beginning of the movie was bright enough to make runway lights for Flynn.

He sidled through the row of people and snagged the seat next to me. I resisted burrowing into him. He had to get settled after all.

With him by my side, I relaxed. His fresh, clean scent was muted by the enticing but subtle smell of his cologne. I liked that fragrance, too, but it wasn't as Flynn as "Flynn at the lake" had been. It was more like his suit. A way to say "I'm a businessman, let's do business." The way Flynn looked, anyone with ovaries would do anything he wanted.

I certainly would.

He gave me a quick smile. I grinned in return. Couldn't help it. I was at the movies. With Flynn. Before he settled back, he dug out a pack of Hot Tamales.

I gasped and whispered, "Thank you." Without thinking, I stretched up to kiss him. I pulled back after a quick peck, second-guessing myself. He wouldn't be here if he weren't interested, right? And he was the one who'd called, so that meant he'd wanted to at least talk to me.

Heat flared in his gaze, the colors from the movie reflecting in his green eyes. In his gaze was a promise that there'd be more than kissing tonight.

Yesss.

His gaze lifted to my headband, which was a yellow tiara with a star in the middle. His lips quirked and he turned his attention to the movie.

I enjoyed my second time through the show more than my first and it wasn't because I was snuggled against a solid wall of warm muscle or munching on my favorite candy. Candy that Flynn had remembered was my favorite.

Credits rolled and I stood and stretched. Flynn rose and eyed my outfit. The yellow W stood out on my red shirt, and I'd bought blue Wonder Woman leggings on sale. His gaze licked the full length of my legs.

"Nice" was all he said before leading me out.

He was a force at my back as we made our way out of the theater and into the hall. Would he stay for the last show? I'd always wanted to do a marathon rewatch for a blockbuster like tonight, but I'd been so focused on saving money. Having him next to me again, drinking in his presence like I'd been on a sugar-free diet for months and he was my personal box of Hot Tamales, I was afraid that if he cocked his head, I'd ditch the show to be with him.

"You were planning to go again?" he asked as if reading my mind. Or was it the needy and desperate look I probably had?

"Yep. I bought all the tickets when I got here." The cashier hadn't even batted an eye. I wasn't in full costume, but my outfit must've said it all.

We reached the hall and held hands to keep from getting separated in the crowd. I was about to break away for the restrooms when a young woman walked up to Flynn, looking at him like he was a full-sized chocolate bunny. He tensed, his shoulders rigid.

A saucy grin formed on her lips. "Heard you were trying to get ahold of me. My sister was so pissed." The woman reminded me of the mean-girl crowd. They all wore the latest trends to perfection, and their cold, haughty stares could drain a girl of self-esteem from twenty paces. It was their superpower.

Wait. Flynn had been trying to call this girl?

I refused to be hurt until I knew the story.

"I, uh. It was resolved." He didn't look at me but scanned the crowd like he was searching for the first exit.

The woman laughed, tossing her long, glossy hair. My next hair appointment should be with a stylist and not at the punch-card place, but not until after I earned my free cut. I was halfway there.

The girl's hip cocked out more. "She said you got stuck with the crazy lady you wanted her to save you from, but I told her I'd make it up to you."

Save him from the crazy lady? Flynn's shoulders drooped and he exhaled. The woman finally noticed me, did a once-over of my outfit, and quirked a brow, as if to ask, *Are you for real?* She turned the wattage of her flirtatious smile up and drifted closer to Flynn.

I still didn't know the whole story, but I wasn't going to stand around and wait for my self-respect to be trampled. I wasn't on this bitch's payroll. "Would that have been Crazy J, Flynn?"

His shoulders hunched more and he dipped his forehead. "Yep. I was trying to save myself from Crazy J." He lifted his gaze but still didn't meet mine. He gripped my hand instead and pulled me closer to him. I went reluctantly, interested to see what he was doing. "You know what, Becky? Thank your sister for doing me a solid and bailing on our deal. Best thing that could've happened." He wrapped his arm around my waist, gave Becky a nod, and hauled me away with him.

To be hurt or not to be hurt? "I need to hear the story. How upset should I be?"

He sighed but held me tighter. "I won't blame you if you hate me. It was a douche move. After you said you were going to bid on me, I called who I thought was Becky, but was her sister, Samantha."

He gave me a sidelong look like he was gauging my reaction.

"I asked her to bid up until she won and I'd cover the cost, no matter the amount. It's understandable, then, that when I kept calling her by her sister's name, she stayed quiet and let you win." He stopped and faced me, his expression serious. "Which I'm grateful for."

"That was such a douche move."

"I know. I'm not proud of my 'genius' plan."

"Not that. Well, that was a douche move, too, but calling her by her sister's name? Ugh. Did you sleep with both of them?"

His face darkened with shame. "Not at the same time."

People flowed around us. Were Becky and her crew part

of the crowd? I didn't care. Hurt roiled under my skin, but he seemed genuinely ashamed of himself. I still wasn't sure what to think now that I had the details.

Why do I always stutter around you? He'd said that out of frustration one day at the cabin. He must've been so desperate to keep out of Crazy J's reach. This whole time I'd been wrapped up in my nightmare at home as a kid, I hadn't dwelled on my effect on Flynn. I'd downright terrified him. So much that ten years later, he'd been willing to fork over as much cash as necessary to save himself from me.

"I'm so sorry."

He recoiled. "For what? I'm the asshole."

"But you wouldn't have been if I hadn't scared you so bad."

"Tilly." His voice dropped to the low rumble that always sent shock waves through my body. When he talked like that, I usually orgasmed hard soon after. "If I hadn't been such a selfish dick, I would've taken the time to get to know you instead of running the other direction. Or doing something stupid like calling an old hookup I never should've led on in the first place."

I licked my lower lip, my skin on fire where he touched. His gaze darted to my tongue, the heat in his eyes matching my own.

Another question pushed to the front of my mind. "Why'd you call? It's been three weeks. I know if you want to get laid, you don't need me." Dare I hope for more? I'd finally pried myself away from my phone after nursing my splintered heart.

His frame went rigid for a heartbeat. "I missed you, and I don't want to have sex with anyone else."

It was a stark confession. The realization bothered him. It was written all over his face. "Does that upset you? Be honest, because I'm too old to be strung along."

I couldn't believe we were having this talk in the movie theater lobby, but I was glad we were having it at all. Because being with him only proved that I refused to go through another three weeks of *will he or won't he*.

He didn't answer right away. Tears pricked the backs of my eyes. No way was I going to cry minutes after watching the same movie back to back about a kick-ass heroine who saved the world.

Tucking a finger under my chin, he raised my face until I met his gaze. "I have a demanding job with asshole clients who think I'm at their command twenty-four seven. And since they're paying me millions, I kind of am. I don't want to jump into a relationship only for you to feel like my job is my mistress. All I know right now is that I can't quit thinking of you and I don't want anyone else."

"I guess we can start there, then." I couldn't escape the feeling that his job was a cop-out, that if he wanted to make it work, he could. But what did I know about running a business of that magnitude? Teaching required a lot of work off-hours, and each hour of tutoring took another hour or two of planning, organizing, and bookkeeping.

Only a couple of people drifted past us now. The next showing would start soon, and it was on the other side of the theater. I tried to lighten the mood. "Now that your dirty secret is out, what do you want to do the rest of the night?"

A flash of alarm crossed his face, but it was gone so fast I must've imagined it. "We have one more movie to watch." He slipped his hand into his pocket and withdrew a ticket stub. "And then I get to show you all the things I've been thinking of since I got home from the cabin."

A thrill shot through me. He'd bought a ticket to watch the 10:15 with me? I could've melted. "And then it'll be my turn!"

Flynn

BY THE TIME we crossed the threshold into her house, I had nearly recreated my first time with Tilly. I'd been with her for hours, unable to talk to her much because of the movie. The quick heart-to-heart conversation between showings had left me emotionally ragged. Especially when she'd said my dirty little secret was out.

By the time she'd joked about racing me back to her place, all I'd wanted was to lose myself in her curves and forget about my shitty past and the dirty deed I had to live with.

I'd taken her against the wall before we'd fallen into her bed. We hadn't done anything more than cuddle since the first frenzied round of sex. I wanted to feel all of her. The terror that had grabbed me by the short hairs and refused to let go as soon as Becky had spoken was still with me.

And then *Tilly* had apologized to *me* for being the one to drive me to such behavior. She was so much better than me.

Could I tell her the truth about my mom and sister one day without fearing she'd lose that look of adoration I'd come to crave?

"What are you thinking about?" she murmured. She was stripped naked and curled into me, her back to my front. My erection pressed between us, but I was content to stroke her silky skin—for now.

"How amazing you are. And that you taste like cinnamon."

She chuckled, making her body shake and teasing my cock. I groaned and snaked an arm around to palm a breast, its weight in my hand better than a stress ball.

"Flynn."

That tone. My happy contentment drained out of me. This was it. She was going to ask about my past.

"You never talk about you."

"There's not much to me." The words rang with truth. Until Tilly had barged back into my life, I'd done nothing more than work and loiter at the clubs until I found someone to stave off the loneliness for a night. Most of the women I met were all decent people. There was the typical mating dance of the human species, one I was tired of. The congenial chatter, the flirtation, the illusion of future possibilities. Women like Becky who were interested in the same no-strings deal I was weren't as satisfying as I'd led himself to believe. Then there were the ones who read into the way I dressed, how freely I spent money on dinner and drinks, what I drove and targeted me.

My only contributions to the world were the buildings I built. For other people.

"What about your family? Was it just you and your sister?"

I didn't answer immediately, just trailed my fingers over her skin while deciding what to tell her. I settled on the majority of the truth. The part I was most ashamed of wouldn't need to be shared. But before I did, I needed her.

Rising over her, I nudged her onto her back. Her look of disappointment stalled me

"One more time first. I promise I'll tell you about my shitty past." Admittedly not as deplorable as hers. But she'd been an innocent victim, at the mercy of those she should've been able to trust with her well-being. I'd failed the one person who should have been able to rely on me for her security. I stroked her face. "I need this. I need you."

She nodded and opened herself to me, cradling me between her legs. I snagged a condom and rolled it on so there'd be no interruptions.

I dipped my head and caught a nipple between my lips. This was my turn to be selfish, to linger over her body, and savor her taste and reaction.

She arched her back as I swirled my tongue, my other hand stroking a path down her stomach, over the rise of her pelvis, until I hit her wet center.

As much as I wanted to plunge inside her welcoming sex, she wasn't ready. I wanted her to fall apart around me as soon as I shoved in. Switching my attention to her other breast, I used the shift to part her folds and rest a finger on her clit.

She undulated against my hand. Always so responsive. Her reaction was real and it made me feel like a god.

One swipe over her nub made her body tremble. I released her nipple and blew across it.

She inhaled. "You're naughty."

"You like it," I growled.

"So much. Do it again."

Uninhibited. Unabashed. My Tilly was the real deal. It had been the real her in high school, too, with a personality so big and bold it'd been like looking at the sun. She never gave up on those she cared for, whether it was the shelter cats or the kids she taught...or me. She humbled me, and she deserved so much better. And dammit, I so wasn't worthy. I was the opposite of the person she tried to be. But for whatever reason, she'd set her sights on me and I couldn't move out of her orbit. I'd made it three weeks without her company, each day an empty husk of existence before I'd run back to steal whatever she was willing to give.

I did as she asked, switching from one breast to the other while sliding my thumb in a steady rhythm over her clit. She was slick with need, her body coiled tight, the tension building.

Her hands gripped my shoulders, nails digging in. Perfection. An unhinged Tilly lay under me, her chest rising and falling in short pants, her hips swiveling, trying to eke out every scrap of pleasure I was giving her.

I slid a finger inside, watched with greedy fascination as she tilted her head back with a groan and arched her luminous breasts closer to me. Her walls clenched my finger. So badly, I wished it was my cock she gripped. Soon.

The first full-body quake hit her. It rippled through her, creating an erotic image I'd remember the rest of my life. This woman drove me crazy in all the good ways.

Slowly, I circled her clit once, twice. Her body tightened. I slid my finger out to replace my thumb on her bundle of nerves. Her eyes flew open as her crest stalled, but I positioned myself and thrust inside. The pressure of my body knocked my finger against her clit and I used the momentum to bring her back to a swift peak.

Holding myself on one shaking arm, I let her passion unfold beneath me.

She cried to the ceiling, she clawed at her bed, she bucked, and when she came, it was the spectacular sight I'd been waiting for. Only then did I let go. The stamina that I normally prided myself on took its own vacation around her. Three thrusts were all I got in before my orgasm hit. Her sex clenched around me, her body cushioning me as I lost myself to blinding ecstasy.

I gave us both time to come down from our peaks, and when our breathing slowed, I rolled off her, dropping a lingering kiss on her lips.

"Let me clean up before we talk."

She returned the kiss but let me go without protest.

In the bathroom, I dropped the condom in the garbage. If I had my way, I'd fill that damn garbage with condom wrappers. Would I seem too needy if I stuck around all weekend? I glanced around the bathroom. It was tidy, old, but well cared for. The rest of the place was the same from the little I'd paid attention on my way to her bedroom. The entire house could fit into my kitchen.

But my place didn't have signs of Tilly everywhere. Like her emoji shower curtain and her pink, plush bathmats. Her towels were just as fluffy and bright yellow, except for the black-and-red one hanging on the hook on the back of her door. It reminded me of her Harley Quinn swimsuit.

And that she was waiting for my life story.

I flicked off the light and opened the door. She was tucked into her bed, facing me.

"Hey," she said. The corner of the blanket flung back. She hadn't dressed, and that fast I could take her again.

"Hey." I crawled in and her gaze dipped to my hardening cock. "I'll be good, I promise."

"Not forever, I hope," she teased.

My stress drained away. Threading an arm under her, I curled her into my chest and planted my gaze on the ceiling. "It was just Lynne and me." How long had it been since I'd said her name out loud? "Growing up was okay. We weren't a perfect family, but who is, I guess. Then the accident happened and my dad died."

Her head popped up. "Your dad drowned, too."

I only nodded. "My mom blamed the world. She'd blamed him for everything. Working too much, not making enough money, having a beater car. But when he died, she never seemed to get past the anger phase of grief. Most of it she redirected at me. School was the only reprieve I got from her relentless hounding. I just couldn't do anything right."

Taking care of my sister as a teenager had been hard enough, but when I was home, I couldn't even sit down. *Change Lynne's diaper, dammit. She pissed herself again. Why didn't you mow the lawn yet? The car's past due for an oil change and I can't fucking afford a service call. Get your ass out there.*

When I looked back, I wondered how I'd tolerated it all. Day after day after day. It had been my life. I'd wallowed in guilt for not being there when Lynne had needed me. The excuse that I'd only been a kid still fell flat. I'd been a stronger swimmer than her and the reality was if I'd been there, at least she'd be alive today. Since Dad had died trying to save her, he'd probably be around, too. Chalk another life onto my conscience.

Why couldn't I have been stronger for Lynne? It was hard to remember her. There'd been nothing left. They'd gotten her breathing again, but she'd suffered a nasty seizure and the resulting brain damage had been hard for a teenage boy to process.

The day I'd walked out the door and never looked back had been the ugliest of them all. I'd gotten home after school —no more sports for me because that took too much time away from being Mom's manservant—and the house had stunk.

Lynne had been parked in her wheelchair alone in front of the TV. Fear had shot through me that our mother had passed, too, and how the hell was I going to care for my sister?

Mom had been asleep in bed while Lynne had festered in her feces for hours.

I'd wrestled my sister into the tub while Mom had hollered about the smell and demanded I take care of it. And I'd tried, but—

With a gruff clearing of my throat, I continued, skipping past the worst. "Without Dad to take the brunt of Mom's unhappiness, she deteriorated. Life was hell and I...left."

I'd almost killed my sister. Left her soaking the dried shit off her skin to go clean up her wheelchair. She'd slid under the water while alone in the bathroom.

Mom's screaming. I squeezed my eyes shut. God. I'd

never hated myself more than that moment, though most days since then had come close.

"My dad's boss never quit checking on me. Abe owned the company I own now, but he built houses, too. That's the company my dad worked for. I had nowhere to go, and I called and asked if he could spot me a night at a motel until I figured the rest out. He and his wife took me in and he gave me a job."

"How old were you."

"Sixteen."

Her warm breath wafted over my chest. "What about your mom now? Is she still alive?"

"Yes. We're estranged."

You get back here and take care of your sister, you spoiled little shit.

Why so you can sleep all day?

Mom hit me up to pay for Lynne's care. Sending her monthly payments for the group home was barely a balm for my troubled soul, but it was all I could bring myself to do. Any more and the price tag was Mom back in my life. I already proved I couldn't care for Lynne.

"Abe put me through school, trained me on the job, and when he died, he left me his business, which I grew and expanded."

"He'd be proud."

I couldn't respond. *Take care of that sister of yours, son. She's got less than you do.*

Somehow, I didn't think Abe would approve of my monthly stipend for Lynne's expenses.

Tilly's breath evened out. I stared at the ceiling. What would Tilly do if she found out I'd abandoned my sister? Tilly, the woman who made it her career to help children.

I'd do my best not to find out.

CHAPTER 11

lynn

RAPPING on the front door had me prying my eyelids open. The first sensation I registered was a firm bottom pressed against my side, then a leg draped over mine. Tilly had rolled over and sprawled in a twist. How could she sleep like that? I was flat on my back but had slept solidly until some asshole had woken me with pounding on a Saturday morning.

The doorbell rang, a sad sound that moaned like it was running low on batteries, only it was electric. Was the wiring bad?

Tilly twitched, her head popped up.

More knocking.

"I'll get it." I'd give it to the bastard, too.

I swung my legs down. My gym bag sat by the front door. Thankfully, I'd had the foresight to bring it in so I didn't have to pull on my slacks. I crept out, checking the door and windows to see if anyone was going to get a view of a full moon in the early morning.

I bent over my duffel and opened it to get my shorts. As I was stepping into them a woman called from the other side. "Tilly? Are you home?"

I ripped open the door, my anger only partially mollified because it was a little old lady disturbing my peaceful morning. "Can I help you?"

The woman paused, her hand poised to knock again, her eyes on my bare chest. It was probably the first time someone other than a bed partner had seen me in a state of disarray. My shorts were rumpled, but my gym was private and in my office building. My hair had to be pointing in every direction from the way Tilly had run her hands through it and fisted it the night before.

Tilly approached from behind. "Hey, Mrs. B."

Mrs. Blumenthal's gaze peeled off my chest. "Tilly. I feared you weren't home. But this young, strapping gentleman answered."

Mrs. B may have been of average height in her prime, but she must be in her eighties now and was closer to five feet tall. Her gaze was as sharp as her mind probably was.

"Flynn, meet my landlady."

I held out my hand. Mrs. B gave me an assessing look as her soft, wrinkled hand clasped mine in a light shake.

She switched her focus to Tilly. Had I passed her inspection? "I wanted to let you know that the roofers aren't going to be here today. You mentioned having to leave while they were working, so I wanted to catch you early."

"Thanks. So when are they going to be here?"

Mrs. Blumenthal heaved a heavy sigh. "I'm going to have to find a new place to do it. The owner of the company kept trying to raise the cost. I showed him the insurance estimate,

I already have twenty percent to pay for the deductible, but he thinks he can con an old woman. Schmuck."

My lips twitched. Abe would've liked Mrs. B.

"I'm sorry." That was the thing about Tilly. She sounded genuinely sorry.

Mrs. Blumenthal waved her off. "It is what it is. I just hope I can get someone before the roof starts leaking. Everyone's booked up after the hailstorm."

I didn't stop to consider what I was offering. "I'll do it."

Both women stared at me. Tilly's smile grew wider by the second.

"Excuse me?" Mrs. Blumenthal turned her head like she was positioning her hearing aid just right.

"I'm a builder. I can do the roof. This weekend, in fact. The weather's supposed to be great." The more I thought about it, the better the idea was. It would be hot, but sunny. The place was small. If I worked today and tomorrow, I could knock it out. "No charge."

Mrs. B's mouth worked. She glanced at Tilly, back at me. "You're a builder?"

"Yes, ma'am." I leaned forward. "It would give Miss Johnson a reason not to kick me out."

Mrs. B harrumphed. "I wouldn't kick you out for eating crackers in bed."

Tilly traced a finger down my abdomen. "Look at these. He doesn't eat crackers."

The ladies cackled and I couldn't stop my smile. "My tools are in my truck. I'll run and grab supplies." I glanced up. "Black shingles?"

"Whatever the hell is up there." She pinned me with a hard look again. "Seriously, though. Don't touch a nail until you tell me how much."

"It's nothing. I don't get my hands dirty nearly enough."

Life had been simpler when I could shut the lid on my toolbox and the day was done.

"I'll vouch for him," Tilly said.

Pride bubbled up. She hadn't seen any of my handiwork, had never seen me hang so much as a picture. But she'd vouched for me. I was going to throw up the best damn roof of my career.

~

Tilly

I crawled into Flynn's pickup. I was more graceful than the first time I'd scaled the distance from the ground to the seat.

"Where are we going first?"

He fired up the engine and backed out of my driveway, which barely fit his massive truck. "We'll hit the home improvement store first. Then I have to run home for my ladder."

I gasped and clapped my hands. "I get to see the Halstengard residence? In person?"

Flynn in his suit, even as casual as he'd been the night before, hadn't matched with the vehicle. But today's shorts and T-shirt fit the image better. The image fit him better, too. What would his house fit with, the suit or the truck?

I still had no clue why he needed such a large vehicle.

His gaze strayed to my legs like they had at the lake. My outfit wasn't crazy on purpose. The clearance-rack workout leggings were covered with large blocks of bold color, but I'd muted it with a black shirt. Not intentionally—it was just an expendable shirt in case it got stained or ripped helping Flynn.

He was helping Mrs. B. He must be terribly generous

with his business, too. With all he had, he must shovel tons over for charity.

He smiled and draped an arm over the steering wheel. "I'm warning you, my house is incredibly nice. Quality-built perfection you'll have a hard time finding anywhere in the great state of Minnesota."

Genuine pride rang in his voice.

"You built it."

He shot me a grin that warmed me more than the late June sun. What would his perfect house look like? I'd never thought of mine. Space would be my first pick. Just space. And a kitchen like the cabin.

"Did you build the cabin, too?"

"No, I haven't dabbled in those. They're not much different, but I moved on to corporate as soon as Abe died."

"When did he pass away?"

"About five years ago, but I was managing his business even during college. His wife wasn't interested, and they had no kids."

"He was lucky to have you."

Flynn's lips flattened. "It was the other way around. I tried to earn my keep. It caused an uproar when I changed the name, but the contractors who'd been with the company for years kept telling me what Abe would do. It was a clear way to tell them who was in charge."

It was hard to see Flynn being a hard-ass. Maybe that was why he'd gone the route of changing the name. I could see him putting in long days. At the cabin, he'd never quit working unless I'd intervened. During our fishing trips and hikes, he'd fidgeted and acted nervously. I'd worried it was him being with Crazy J, but no, it was him having work withdrawals.

We pulled up to the home improvement store. It was no

massive box store. The building he'd parked in front of was a quarter of the size of Home Depot.

I got out and followed him inside. A woman my mom's age greeted Flynn with a hearty hug. His answering grin was genuine.

"Tilly, this is Dorothy, an old friend of Abe's."

Dorothy shook her hand. "There were some years if I didn't have Abe's business, I had nothing. Whatcha need, Flynn?"

He ran through a list of supplies and we cruised around the store, gathering nails, tubes of stuff, and other things while Flynn and Dorothy chattered in what seemed like a different language.

Dorothy rushed to the back of the store. "Pull around back and we'll load the shingles."

I followed Flynn out. "Aren't we going to pay?"

"Dorothy'll bill me." He walked with easy confidence, looking like a guy out for a basketball game, more relaxed than I'd seen him. He was in his element. Dorothy was one of his people. How many others like her did he have in his life?

Once the shingles were loaded, he took off for his place. He crossed through town and hit the 494.

"You don't live in Minneapolis?"

"Chanhassen."

He'd told me he'd built his house, but I still pictured him in a top-floor condo with glass walls and a view of the city. "Wow, that's a nice area. You really are like Bruce Wayne, then? Massive manor, bat caves hidden on the property. Do you have a butler?"

"I have a cleaning service and a personal chef. I don't get company, so no Alfred."

"I have a hard time believing you don't get company." She poked him in the side. "Someone had to let Becky in."

He grunted and scowled at me. "I don't have women over, either. It was…"

I narrowed my gaze on him. "Go on."

He gripped the steering wheel, his knuckles turning white. "It was easier if they didn't know where I lived."

"Solid plan." I snorted. "You don't have a personal assistant that'll 'take out the trash' like Iron Man?"

A grudging smile lit his face. "No Pepper working for me, no. Though I'm sure neither Matthew nor his husband would object to kicking out anyone I asked them to. In fact, he gets frustrated if I don't give him more to do."

"You're a total control freak." When he turned down a long drive, I sat forward and slammed my hands on the dash. To Flynn's credit, he didn't jump. "This is your house? Get. Out."

A sprawling three-story house that had to appraise in the millions was spread before us. Rock accents matched perfectly with the white trim and dark blue siding. I lost count of the arches, but every room inside must have a peaked ceiling.

And the landscaping. June was the heart of summer, and a rich green lawn surrounded the house and outbuildings that matched the style of the home. Neatly trimmed bushes lined the driveway and smaller manicured bushes rimmed the walkway to the house. To one side, a fountain spewed water next to a wide expanse of lush grass that made me itch to kick off my shoes and frolic. I might have to do that before we left.

He pulled along the driveway to a garage that took up one entire side of the massive structure. The wider of the four garage doors, doors that were nicer than any door I'd ever seen, lifted to reveal an open-bay garage.

"You do have a Batmobile." I couldn't identify the sports

car, but it was sleek, black, and probably did zero to sixty in four seconds—if that was good for a car. I had no idea.

Flynn chuckled and parked. "Sometimes I need better gas mileage."

He hopped out. I slid down. This garage didn't have the musty, cracked-floor smell of my rental's garage. There was also enough room for me to fully open the door and not have to slither against the wall. I could park another vehicle next to his truck and hang all the doors open and they still wouldn't touch.

I couldn't help myself. I wandered outside into the sun as he loaded a ladder in the bed of his pickup, which was now full. And that was why he drove such a massive truck.

The weather beckoned me. Sunny, a light breeze, there was nothing more summery than the smell of a freshly cut lawn. I toed off my shoes, rolled off my socks, and scurried across the driveway.

"Holy shit." I stopped to inspect the surface. "Even your concrete is fancy." The surface had been pressed and polished until it resembled cobblestone.

Flynn's athletic shoes came into view as I felt up his pavement. "There's a new company in town that does this. They gave me a deal. It was the biggest project they've ever done. And it's good business for them; they can say they did a job for the owner of Halstengard Industries."

I straightened. His green eyes paled in the sun, almost iridescent. "You like helping the underdog."

"I don't do much," he muttered.

I popped up on my toes and gave him a quick kiss. "Now excuse me while I go feel up your lawn." Spinning, I sprinted away.

The second my feet left the warm concrete and hit cool grass, I could've collapsed and sighed. Mrs. B hired mowers and that was as much care as my tiny stretch of lawn got. All the mowers did was beat back the weeds. I doubted there was much grass left to grow after years of neglect.

Throwing my hands in the air, I ran and twirled. "This is so fun!" I should probably stop because we had work to—

A solid force tackled me from behind.

I didn't hit as hard as I feared. Flynn's arm banded around me to cradle me to his chest as he lowered us.

"You drive me crazy." His voice was gruff, his hands lifting my shirt.

Breathing hard, I only helped him. "I couldn't resist."

"Come here anytime and do that." He kissed me hard and released me to yank my shirt off. "But be warned, it gets me hot as fuck."

I reached for the bulge in his shorts and palmed him. He groaned and pushed down my bottoms.

"How are we…" There was nothing but grass, and it was a highly maintained lawn, but to have sex on it?

He ripped open a condom packet. "Hands and knees."

I jutted my chin toward the wrapper he'd tossed next to us. "Invisible utility belt?"

"Never leave home without it. Kneel."

Ooh, I liked bossy Flynn. I did as ordered, falling to my hands. He rolled my leggings just past my ass, limiting my mobility.

Strong hands grabbed my hips and a rush of desire came with his touch. He was intense, demanding, and I liked this side of Flynn as much as when he was frantic to get inside of me.

Straddling my legs, he parted me and pushed inside. I was already wet enough for him, no foreplay other than him tackling me required.

He took me hard and rough. His hands didn't leave my hips. He didn't whisper words of beauty or love. He just drove into me over and over.

It was perfect. The hard smack of his balls was all the stimulation my clit needed. I reached my peak and fisted grass.

"Flynn. Harder."

He complied. I bowed my back to open up for him. Grass ripped from the lawn. I grabbed more. He pounded me until I screamed his name.

With a roar, he arched back behind me, his cock jerking and pulsing. We finished together.

He sagged over me, still seated inside. "Fuck, that was intense."

"Next time," I panted, "I'm shouting Puddin' all over the yard."

His dick twitched inside of me. "I'm never going to get the roof started if you keep talking like that. But just in case, plan to do it next Saturday."

"Deal."

He withdrew and covered himself with his shorts before helping me straighten my clothing and stand. I glanced around. Trees surrounded his place, granting us the privacy I didn't think about until now. With a display of unexpected intimacy, he cupped my chin and pressed a soft kiss to my lips.

"Wanna back the truck out and shut the door? I need to change into my work clothes."

As we walked back to the house, hand in hand, I couldn't stop my grin. He'd tried to forget me for weeks, but within hours, he'd introduced me to his people, brought me to his house, and even trusted me with his expensive ride. If only I could go back to my sixteen-year-old self and tell her not to worry, it'd all be okay. She'd get the guy after all.

Flynn

I FOUGHT to hold still as Tilly dabbed aloe gel on my shoulders. I hissed and jerked away, then sighed and relaxed back. Each new spot she spread the green goop, I reacted the same way.

"We underestimated the power of the sun." She spread the gel around to cover the angry red sunburn.

"And how the black shingles amplify it. I baked myself." I'd put on sunblock but worked through the day without stopping to reapply it.

Squirting more aloe gel into her hand, she covered me with another coat. Her touch was light, and for the first time in a long while, I didn't want her pressed against me. Having her around was fun, though. She'd also spent a lot of time outside bringing me refreshments and running tools up the ladder.

The roof was done and it was almost suppertime. I'd worked late last night and then been up and hammering away this morning as soon as we'd had another round—that ended up being two—of sex. I was tempted to bring her to my house, where I could fill my tub with tepid water to soothe my inflamed skin, then have her crawl in with me.

She tossed the gel aside and sat back on the couch. "You haven't mentioned going for a run once all weekend."

I shrugged and winced. "I don't need to when I do this work all day."

"So being in an office stresses you out? You don't enjoy it."

"Why do you say that?" Was it that obvious? I grabbed her remote to flip the TV on. She had no cable. I scanned through the stations she did get. Nothing.

"Just how you acted on vacation. On day one, I thought you were going to work the whole week, but by day seven, you never touched your laptop. Then this weekend. You were still in your suit after most offices had been closed for hours."

That was my life. "There's not a damn thing on." I tossed the remote down. "Do you have any movies?"

She gave me a droll look and pointed to the box by the TV. "Pick your poison. Michael Keaton Batman, post–Michael Keaton inferior-nineties Batman, Christian Bale Batman—my favorite—or Ben Affleck Batman. Or we can change it up. CGI *Green Lantern* or *Deadpool*. How about Marvel? I've got Tobey Maguire Spider-Man or Andrew Garfield Spider-Man. Or the new guy. You'd be surprised how quickly newly released DVDs end up at the thrift store. I love it. If you're not in a superhero mood, I found the whole series of *Downton Abbey* at a pawnshop. We can learn the fine art of insults from the dowager countess."

"Who?" I shook my head. "Never mind, I'll go with new-guy Spider-Man."

I was crawling to the box to dig the movie out when the faint chime of music caught my attention. "Is that your phone?"

"Hmm?" She pried her gaze off my ass in my carpenter jeans. I was man enough to admit that I relished the way she checked me out in my work clothes.

The theme song to *My Little Pony* played from the kitchen. For a moment, I was transported back to childhood, watching cartoons while Lynne belted out the song. My throat constricted. I never remembered the good times anymore.

"Oh shit." She ran to grab it and I stuffed away my emotions and kept looking for the movie.

The movie was in and set up. Tilly's voice resonated from the kitchen in strangely even, though upbeat tones. Work call?

I eased back onto the couch, careful of my shoulders. Glancing around her small living room, I mentally tallied all the projects I could do. Repaint the ceiling—water damage had seeped through at some point. The entire place could use a fresh coat of paint, in something other than primer white. Every window could be replaced. The house was over forty years old. The carpet and laminate weren't original, but they were still outdated. I didn't have to use the appliances to know they were old and sucked energy.

If I had a place like this, I'd have weekend projects for a year.

Tilly rushed out, her face bright with excitement. I smiled just watching her. Her shorts today were a vivid purple with yellow trim and her white shirt didn't hide her fuchsia bra.

"I have a new client!" She bounced on the couch, but far enough away she didn't jostle the fabric against my skin.

"Awesome." Anything more than word-of-mouth advertising probably wasn't in her budget. For new clients to find her, she had to be good. I didn't have to see her work to know she was amazing at her job. Her caring and enthusiasm were obvious.

"They want twice a week, even through the school year. I can't wait to meet the girl."

"You're okay working all day with kids and then tutoring at night?" And she said I put in long days.

She lifted a shoulder. "It's fun. I won't lie, it can be tiring. It sounds clichéd, but teaching is very rewarding."

I could make a list of why my work was rewarding and it'd be laughable next to hers. "You're a good person."

She smiled and snuggled into me. I didn't mind the sting when I put my arm around her.

"So are you." She dropped a kiss on my chest.

I punched start for the movie. "No. I'm not."

Trailing her fingers along the ridges of my stomach, she

met my gaze. "Why wouldn't you think so? You do a lot for others. Seriously, you'd have to hurt a kid for me to hate you." She switched her attention to the TV.

Mom's screams rang as clear as the day it had happened. *You almost killed your sister again!*

CHAPTER 12

lynn

I WRAPPED up a call with a prospective client looking to build a large-format retail store. That was one thing Minneapolis and the surrounding areas didn't slack in. Winning bids and finishing projects would keep me at the top. Clients loved that I was local, a homegrown kid, and it helped that Abe had built a prime reputation during his years. I was using that momentum to bid for educational facilities. The way the population grew, I'd never run out of work between retail, new builds, and renovation projects for schools and athletic facilities. It'd been a market I'd set my sights on as soon as I gained control.

A message from my executive assistant popped up on the monitor. *Someone brought you lunch? But she's not leaving.*

Dammit. I jumped up. No one knew I was seeing anyone and my assistant was ferocious about who gained access to my office. My personal assistant was almost as bad. If Matthew ever got ahold of Tilly, she'd get an interrogation just short of violent.

Tilly had commented that I probably worked through lunch. And yes, if I didn't have a meet and greet over a meal, it's not like I packed anything. I hadn't thought she was serious about bringing me food.

I rushed to the door and took a second to smooth my clothes and check my hair. It wouldn't do to let my staff see me lose my cool over Tilly.

I froze with my hand on the doorknob. It was Monday. Wacky Monday. Oh god, what if she was dressed for it?

Did it matter?

No. But my heart rate didn't get the message.

I opened the door in a smooth motion. Tilly, dressed in jean shorts and a plain purple top, stared out the window, commenting on the view. Professional pride spiked. I had been with Abe when he'd picked this location for his new office building, using it as his gateway into corporate construction, proof of his abilities. Our offices took up the top two floors. The four floors below us were filled with financial advisers, lawyers, and various consultants. Many of them I used in my own business if I didn't staff them already.

"I mean, look at that sky." Tilly's breath fogged the window. My assistant, Mrs. Silverstein, tightened her hand around her pen. "It's like there's not even glass here, it's so clear."

"Not anymore," Mrs. Silverstein said evenly. Tilly took an abrupt step back and clasped her hands behind her back.

I was caught between irritation at my assistant for making Tilly feel unwelcome and my need to rescue Tilly without making a scene. "What's that delicious smell?"

Tilly spun around a wide smile on her face. That grin was

fast becoming the reason I looked forward to each day. Her laughter buoyed my spirit after days of catering to people, trying to win their business, and be congenial and efficient enough to have them recommend me to others. The three weeks after vacation had been Groundhog Day, the same routine over and over again. Even if my actions weren't identical to those of the day before, my goals and outlook for each day were.

In contrast, the three weeks after tracking Tilly down at the movies had been a blur. I'd delegated more duties to both my personal and executive assistants, receiving inquiring looks that I ignored. Work still went late, but I was out of the office by eight p.m. at the latest. Tilly didn't tutor past seven, and I had a driving need to taste her every night, even if we fell into bed without having sex.

Tilly adjusted a narrow headband that shone suspiciously like a small tiara. "I made chicken alfredo, but I left the pasta out of yours. So really, you get chicken and sauce."

My stomach rumbled as soon as she finished the description. Tilly picked up her tote bag full of food and shot Mrs. Silverstein a smile. The woman's lips were pursed, and her gaze darted from the food to Tilly to her tiara.

"I'm sorry, Mr. Halstengard. I didn't realize you were expecting company." Ah, so Mrs. Silverstein was more upset that I hadn't updated her on my plans than how Tilly looked or acted. I hoped.

I inclined my head. As much as I respected Mrs. Silverstein, she could be overbearing. She was no-nonsense, and after having raised five boys, she didn't put up with much bullshit, even from me. All traits I normally appreciated and relied upon. But when it came to my personal life, I... couldn't figure out why I was so defensive about Tilly.

"Thank you, Mrs. Silverstein." I gave Tilly a reassuring

smile. "Come on in, Tilly." I placed a hand on the small of her back and led her in.

"Ohmigosh. I almost got stopped at the front door because they thought I was delivering the pizzas they'd ordered. Then her. I thought she was going to haul me out by force. I was like, seriously, just ask him if I can visit."

I guided her to my conference table. She set the bag down and started setting out the stuff. Her mouth was set in a line and hurt glimmered in her eyes.

"Did she insult you?" I asked sharply.

"No. It's nothing. Just not what I expected when I wanted to bring you lunch."

"I'm sorry. I forgot you even mentioned it, or I would've informed Mrs. Silverstein."

"No problem." Tilly dished out our food. She slapped chicken and peas on my plate, while hers steamed with fresh pasta mixed with grilled chicken.

I wolfed down my food, hungrier than expected, unable to keep my eyes from coveting her pasta. She munched on hers, not eating with her normal gusto.

"What's wrong?" I asked.

She pushed her plate away, her eyes downcast. "She didn't know who I was."

"I don't talk about my personal life with my staff." I hadn't had much of a personal life before summer started.

"Your assistant—what's his name?"

"Matthew."

"Yeah, Matthew. He was leaving for lunch and Mrs. Silverstein asked him if you'd ever mentioned me." She folded her hands in her lap, looking more solemn than I'd ever seen. "What are we?"

"We're...us." My food turned to lead in my gut. Hot, savory food that she'd cooked just for me. Then brought here and gotten deeply insulted for the trouble.

Her gray gaze lifted to mine. "What is 'us'? Are you still ashamed of me?"

I failed her. I failed her hard. All I had to do was mention to either Matthew or Mrs. Silverstein that I was dating someone and they wouldn't have given Tilly such a hard time. I got down on my knees and crept toward her. She didn't move, but she didn't reach for me.

"Tilly, before you, I had no one to talk about. I made sure I had no one to talk about. My focus has been on this company and keeping it thriving. This relationship is new territory for me."

"You still didn't answer." She stroked my cheek, her look sober. "Are you ashamed of me?"

I recalled my first thought after she'd arrived. Wacky Monday. It was a reflex, an echo of me before I was the lucky bastard that got to know her. "Of course not. I'm a private man."

"I don't want to be your Crazy J again." Her hand trembled. This was upsetting her.

I wasn't ashamed of her; I was ashamed of myself for not being strong enough, thoughtful enough, to keep her from feeling this way. I dragged her to the edge of her chair and closer to me. "Hey. It turns out my Crazy J was a pretty phenomenal girl and I was an ignorant idiot."

She softened under my touch. "Are you sure this was okay?"

"Yes." I kissed her forehead, then her cheek. "I'll check my schedule and you can bring me lunch whenever I don't have a meeting." I made my way to her lips.

She kissed me back and I couldn't keep myself from deepening the kiss. I swept my tongue along the seam of her mouth until she opened for me. *Yes.* Blood raged through my veins, careening to my groin.

I wanted her naked, and I wanted her now.

"Flynn," she murmured. "We can't do this in your office."

"I'm the boss." I tugged at her waistband.

She looked around. My windows filled an entire wall on two sides and were reflective enough that no one could see in.

While she was deciding, I freed my shaft and dug out protection—so I was ready if she said yes. For good measure, I flung my tie over my shoulder.

She turned her bright gaze on me. That was what I wanted to see. Excitement and desire instead of shame.

"You're so hot," she growled and yanked me toward her by the shirt.

I couldn't tell her, or anyone else in words, what she meant to me, but I proceeded to show her while she opened me up to the possibilities of office sex.

∼

Tilly

I VEERED AROUND MY ROOM. "Pants. Pants. Pants." Hanging with Flynn all weekend had left me low on laundry, but I hadn't wanted to miss one second of the positions we'd come up with in his hot tub.

Coming back to my house after a weekend at his bachelor pad was like zooming out 200 percent. My rental had never seemed small before. When I showered at Flynn's, it was certainly noticeable when I forgot to get a towel ready. In my place, all I had to do was lean out and grab it off the rack. I could also courtesy flush the toilet from anywhere in the bathroom. At Flynn's place, his toilet had its own freaking room.

It was fun for a weekend. Living the high life. With Flynn.

I dug through my dirty laundry basket. My khaki slacks were rumpled, but they'd smooth out in this humidity. I gave them a sniff.

Meh, good enough. Only me and Charlie had to suffer through them for an hour. And maybe they'd repel his dad.

I sped to the Woods' place and parked in my usual spot. Rushing to the door, I hummed to myself. A tendril of anxiety crept through the warm sun and cool breeze, unsettling the euphoria from my weekend.

I knocked on the door.

And waited.

And waited. Any longer and I'd be officially late. Not good in Mrs. Woods's eyes, who wouldn't listen to the "no one answered the door for me" excuse.

Berta finally opened. Her expression was the most serious I had ever seen and she wouldn't meet my gaze.

"Berta? What's wrong?" I was about to step forward and embrace the woman. Sadness emanated from her so strongly, it was like the sun had dimmed a few thousand watts.

Berta shook her head. Mr. Woods appeared behind the woman, his face stern, his suit buttoned, and not a hair out of place.

"Tilly. You won't be needed today."

Berta let out a strangled cry and shoved away from us. I peered after her, then cast a questioning look at Mr. Woods.

"Did something happen? Is Charlie okay?"

He rose another inch as if lording over me. "You of all people should know that answer." I cocked my head, opened my mouth to ask him what he meant, but he talked over me. "Your services won't be needed here any longer. You're fired, Miss Johnson."

"What? Why?"

The door slammed in my face. I jumped back lest it hit my nose.

Fired?

The first feeling that emerged beyond confusion was relief. No more Mrs. Woods.

Then shame flooded me. No more Charlie. I wasn't arrogant enough to think that I was the best one to help him, but I was good, dammit. Awesome at my job. I had a connection with the boy, a trust we'd built.

No more chats with Berta. But no more dodging Mr. Woods's advances. And no more steady client.

I sighed and strode back to my car. The mother who'd called to hire me last week would help fill the pay gap. Still, I hated to lose the account.

All businesses had setbacks, and if I was going to lose someone, the Woods were a good choice. They had found me through word of mouth from another client, so as long as I hadn't done anything to get blacklisted, I was good.

The drive home was filled with more pondering. It was harder not knowing why I'd been fired.

I arrived home and parked. Worrying my lower lip, I glowered out of the window. How rude and unprofessional of Mr. Woods to treat me like that! No explanation. No notice. This was my livelihood. I wasn't stupid rich like the Woods.

What an ass.

Before I got out, I dug through my tote for my phone. What was Flynn doing tonight? Would he care to hear about my woes?

Missed calls popped up on the screen. Dammit. I shut my ringer off when I was working.

I recognized two of the numbers as current clients. One had left a message.

"Hi, Tilly. I'm sorry. Um…we're going to have to cancel all of our sessions. Your services are no longer required."

Services no longer required? What was going on?

A text popped up from one of the missed calls. *Please don't come tomorrow. Or any other day. We're done with tutoring.*

Another one?

Tears sprang up. I sniffled. The tiny empire I'd busted my ass to build was crumbling and I had zero idea why.

Pulling up the first missed number, I called. Fire me over voicemail? Where was the respect?

"Miss Johnson." The grim tone of one of my favorite clients didn't bolster my confidence.

"Mr. Graham, hi. Can you let me know why you've decided to part ways?" I fiddled with my hair and racked my brain for ways to sound professional and not desperate. "I strive to keep improving my business and your feedback is valuable." Because I'd lost three accounts in an hour.

Mr. Graham huffed. "I can't imagine why I have to explain. The safety of our daughter is our utmost concern."

"Why would you—"

"Look, Miss Johnson, I'm not going to sit and debate this. I can't have a woman suspected of beating a kid allowed to be alone with mine."

The air *whooshed* out of my lungs. *"What?"*

But Mr. Graham had hung up.

I sucked in a sharp breath. And another. If I kept doing it, I'd hyperventilate.

Hyperventilating sounded good right now.

Beating a kid?

Who? When?

I dialed the client who'd left the text. They didn't answer.

Dare I call Mr. Woods and ask for his specific reasoning? *You of all people should know the answer.* And he'd slammed a door in my face. A guy like him didn't think he needed to answer to anyone.

Beat a kid?

I grabbed my tote and stomped into the house. My phone buzzed. I fumbled to answer it.

"This is Tilly."

"Oh…Uh, Miss Johnson. This is Samantha Kringle, we talked last week."

I pinched the bridge of my nose before I let out a giant sob. "Yes, Ms. Kringle. How are you?"

"Good. Well, I called to say we've reconsidered our need for tutoring. I'm afraid we're not interested after all."

I struggled to dam my tears. I shook from the effort. Squeezing my eyes shut, I asked, "Please be honest about why you're not interested. There seems to be something circulating about me and no one will clue me in."

There was a beat of silence. "Well, the friends who recommended you said another family they know became suspicious when their son developed sores and bruises after your sessions."

Charlie? "And they thought I was hitting him? That's a lie." He had been injured before my time with him.

"I—I don't know what to believe. But I'm sure you can understand the position it puts parents in. We'll have to find a new tutor. Goodbye, Miss Johnson."

I tossed her phone on the couch and shrieked, releasing a well of fury and frustration. Instead of questioning me, Mr. Woods had fired me and then spread the word to other clients, who'd told other friends they'd recommended me to.

I now had no summer income. The three other families I worked for would can me as soon as I explained what was happening. And Ms. Kringle was correct. If I was a parent, I'd be overly cautious about protecting my kids from the ugliness I'd endured.

There was no way Mr. Woods would find enough proof to press charges. I'd done nothing but teach and nurture Charlie.

But so much damage had been done. I'd have to be honest with my full-time job, too, and let the principal know what was going on. Then I'd probably lose my position at the school.

I sank into the sofa and sobbed.

CHAPTER 13

lynn

THE RESTAURANT BUSTLED WITH ACTIVITY. Fluorescent lights lit the mirrored columns and reflected off counters in contrast with the exposed brick walls, giving the bar an ultra-hip vibe. It wasn't one of my favorite places. Young entrepreneurs like me swaggered from the entrance, to table, to barstool. They talked loudly, guffawed unnecessarily, and preened at their reflections.

I was one of them, but lately, I'd felt disconnected from locales like this. John Woods probably thrived in an environment like this, where boasting and pontificating was a pastime meant to drive the career train further and harder.

I glanced at Tilly. She poked at her food with a fork. All the fire had been drained out of her and I'd hated bringing her here, but I'd been swamped in work when she'd called last night. I'd rushed over in time to hold her as she cried herself to sleep.

Some asshole had accused her of abusing a child.

The rage set my teeth on edge. I was 120 percent positive that the accusations were false. Why would someone destroy her life like that? She'd worked so hard for everything. It'd be like someone flouncing in and dismantling my construction empire with nothing but rumors.

I'd had another full schedule today but had Mrs. Silverstein clear a couple of meetings and I coaxed Tilly out for food. Then John Woods had called for another meeting over drinks. The guy was getting relentless like he wanted me to be his wingman ever since the nanny had quit or gotten fired because maybe Mrs. Woods wasn't as clueless as her husband thought she was.

Tilly didn't need to suffer a place like this, but I wouldn't be done until who knew what hour, and it'd be too late to make sure she'd taken care of herself. This way, she met me here and got out of her house, and I could still have my meeting.

A stranger wouldn't know anything was wrong, but I did. Seeing her so dejected tore me up, no matter what she wore. Her butter-soft leggings with the Wonder Woman logo on them must've come from Arcadia. Mara wore similar ones. Tilly's shirt was oversized and as bold as Tilly usually was.

Not today.

The ensemble didn't stop the business-formal crowd from ogling her. The men's gazes traveled up and down her legs. Like me, they probably envisioned peeling them down and uncovering the present underneath. I made sure to glare each one down. The women, too, if their gaze was anything beyond, *hey, where did she get those awesome leggings?*

Tilly set her fork down with a resigned sigh.

"You don't like the chicken?" I asked. She didn't have much time to eat before John arrived. Tilly didn't need to deal with his presence, and I didn't feel like warding off comments from the guy. I couldn't delude myself into thinking that the man would quit with sexual references when he saw I was taken. John was married and open, to me at least, about his trysts with the nanny. He could be lying, but I doubted it. Men like John didn't have to lie. They had the looks and the money and knew how to target those with similar ambitions or morals.

It was likely what had attracted John to me.

I scowled across the bar at that thought.

I hadn't been the only company bidding for the project. An international corporate construction company had fought hard for John's business, but I had wined and dined the man while pushing my company hard. *We're local. I understand what you need.*

Had John only seen a young man willing to sell out for money?

No. Because that wasn't me. No matter my personal life, I made sure my work was tight and defensible. I'd sell out for my company. There's a difference.

"I'm just not hungry." Tilly caught the server. "May I get a to-go box?"

Tilly slumped in her seat after the server left. "You don't mind, do you? I don't want to waste your money, but I also need to be thrifty since I have no income." Her eyes glistened.

"Tilly…" What could I say? *It sucks. Shit happens but you'll get through this. Look at everything you've gone through. You got this.* It all sounded inane. Her career was destroyed, and she had nothing to fall back on.

"So I've been looking up legal jargon. I haven't been arrested yet and I think that's a good sign."

"I can always help with that, get a recommendation from my legal team for a good lawyer."

Hope infused her gaze and it was the most life I'd seen out of her since the weekend. Then she glanced at her phone. "Oh, I gotta get going. I don't want to tank your career, too."

I shook my head to tell her not to worry, but then my gaze caught on a man striding through the restaurant, an arrogant smile on his face as he checked out a millennial with mile-long legs sticking out from her skirt. Damn, he was early.

John jutted his chin up when he saw me.

"I'm sorry, Tilly. My client's here. And don't worry about food. I'm not going to let you starve."

"Oh, no problem." Tilly gathered her tote. "Anyway, he can ruin my career, but I don't think he can get me arrested."

John drew even with the table, the arrogance fading from his expression the closer he got until it morphed into menace. "I wouldn't be so sure about that, Miss Johnson."

Color leeched from Tilly's face. My stomach bottomed out.

These two knew each other? And what the hell had John's comment meant?

"Mr. Woods?" Tilly's eyes widened, a mixture of emotions making her irises gray. She turned her stare on me. "You two know each other?"

"This is who I was meeting," I said.

A cruel sneer twisted John's face. "I can't stand even looking at you, Miss Johnson, but I shouldn't be talking to you. My lawyer might be upset with me."

Oh *shit*. John Woods was the guy accusing Tilly of child abuse? How could that be?

A cold wave of dread washed through me as I sat by and watched the two interact.

"Your lawyer," Tilly sputtered. "Wasn't scaring all my business away enough for you? How could you think I'd do something like that to Charlie?"

"I didn't at first, I'll be honest. But the week you were on vacation, he was fine. You come back, and he has black-and-blue marks all over his torso. I guess the 'he hit his head during one of his fits' excuse only worked a couple of times."

"I only helped Charlie. I would never hurt anyone." She rose to face John. I made to stand, but John held up a hand, his gaze calculating.

"Have a seat and let me tell you both how it's going to go."

I bristled at the man's tone, but John didn't operate by the same moral compass as everyone else. I had Abe's advice running in a steady stream through my head about everything, but my mind was silent. What would Abe say about my largest account ruining my girlfriend's life?

I pulled Tilly down in the chair next to me. She stiffened at the force and I lightened my hold. To not hear what John had to say would be stupid. The entitled prick was like an evil villain in a TV show, monologuing his plan to show her how much smarter he was.

John sat across from us, his face as cold as when he'd worked up the contract for his new bank. "I'm surprised to see you two together."

"I didn't hurt Charlie," Tilly said through gritted teeth.

John rolled a hard gaze toward her. "As you know, he's nonverbal and can't speak for himself. Therefore, he can't tell me what you did. But since I contribute considerably well to the officer's association and the county attorney is an old frat buddy, they're listening closely to what I have to say. In four instances, my son had injuries after your visit. In two cases, you even cared for them and played them off as results of his condition. A truly deplorable tactic."

She clutched her hands around her tote. "It wasn't me. And a deplorable tactic is trying to get an innocent person arrested and not find out what really happened."

I rested my hand on hers. There was no way Tilly could afford an attorney. I was on the verge of offering my help, but as soon as I did, I'd burn any dealings with John Woods to ash. The repercussions could be as devastating as what Tilly was going through. Only her business employed one person. I employed hundreds. I had to think through what exactly I could do.

The action didn't escape John's notice. "Mr. Halstengard, I certainly hope you don't plan to use your access to a team of lawyers to aid Miss Johnson in her fight. I can't imagine the public taking kindly to such a prominent businessman helping a child abuser."

"John—" I didn't like threats, but the undertone of John's words was clear. Help Tilly and he'd launch a smear campaign.

John's sharp gaze darted between me and Tilly. "What a small world. It makes sense, I guess. Do you know why I chose your company, Flynn? Because it was local. Because I looked into your past and knew that if you ever tried to fuck with me, I could just tell my good friend at the TV station about how you run a multimillion-dollar corporation, yet your sister's in a state-run home, receiving not a dime from her dear brother."

My world slowed. The thump of my heart grew until it drowned out all other sounds. I withdrew my hand from Tilly's.

Struggling to regain mental equilibrium, bits of information flowed in. John knew about Lynne. Now Tilly knew I lied.

But John had said "state-run home." Lynne was supposed to be in a four-bed group home not far from Mom. A private-run facility she had complained cost a couple of grand a month.

"I thought your sister died." Tilly's soft voice broke through my haze.

I dragged my gaze to hers, so full of confusion and

infusing quickly with betrayal as the realization that I'm a shit liar at the very least and a calloused and cold-hearted brother at the worst.

There was no way to explain and come out the good guy —because I wasn't a good guy. Walking away from Lynne and trusting my mother to do right by her was deplorable. I should've followed up when I got on my feet instead of shoving money at Mom to assuage my guilt.

"Tilly, I—"

John laughed, the sound full of scorn. "That's rich. When I saw you together, I thought you'd bonded over your mutual mistreatment of the disadvantaged."

≈

Tilly

"Flynn?" I tried again.

Mr. Woods and his superiority complex grated on my nerves on a normal day. He turned his snide gaze on me. "Died? No, she suffered brain damage from a boating accident. Flynn here hasn't had a thing to do with her since."

"That's not true," Flynn bit out. His color was returning, but the answer dulled the brilliant color of his eyes. The panic of John's statement was fading, remorse setting in. For lying to me? Or for his alive and maybe not well sister?

"Then when are you around her? When you put her in the home? Is that what you think I should do with my son. Throw him away and forget about him? How nice of you and your mother to let the taxpayers foot the bill. I'm sure future clients will think you're the guy to entrust with all their money on a project."

His sister was alive? He'd let me believe she'd drowned, but she'd survived and not without major complications. State-run group home? When Flynn had a house bigger than any of the group homes I had ever seen? He could employ his own staff just for his sister, but he'd carved her out of his life.

Mr. Woods switched his attention to me and I tensed. "And you, Miss Johnson. I've already investigated your past. I should've done a more thorough job before my wife hired you, but finding someone for Charlie was so difficult." Regret rippled over his face. The man was a complete bastard, but he cared about his son. If only he'd find out who'd hurt Charlie. "But if you think about tapping into your boyfriend's legal resources, think about how it will look for a girl whose own parents are scared of her."

"What?" Several heads turned our way at my shout. How could he bring up my parents? They were only scared of me because I was an adult now and not under their guardianship. The thought would almost be laughable if my abuse hadn't been so severe.

"I had my investigator track them down. They had a lot to say. Killing stray cats? Miss Johnson, I won't stop until you're locked away for a long time. No one hurts my family." He knocked on the table in front of a stunned Flynn. I flinched. "Tread carefully. I will not let my family and everything I've worked for suffer for two hateful individuals."

He got up, straightening his suit with curt, practiced actions, and eyed us both before striding away.

I squeezed the handles of my tote and looked at Flynn. "He's a monster."

Flynn nodded absently, his gaze on the tabletop.

Had Mr. Woods been the one beating Charlie?

No. I hadn't gotten that sense from him. With all the anger radiating off of him, I would've crawled under the table if I'd sensed violence. A man like him bullied with the force of his resources, not his body.

I didn't hit Charlie. I'd figure out how to deal with the accusations later. I had another mess to sort.

"What's the story with Lynne?" It couldn't be true. Flynn was too caring to leave his sister floundering. He'd described his mom as a bitter, awful person. He wouldn't leave someone who couldn't help themselves with someone like that. Would he?

"It's, uh..." He sighed and scrubbed his face with his hands, then slumped in his seat. "It's exactly as he said. I left home and never looked back. I send money to Mom for Lynne's care."

"You send money," I echoed. "You pay her off to not bother you with her?"

"No." His voice lacked conviction.

"Mr. Woods is right?" I shivered, hating how the man could be so wrong about me but perhaps not about Flynn. I thought of something else the vile man said. "Is he also right that you'd protect your deal with him over me?"

"I..." Flynn raised his tortured gaze to mine. "This is so much bigger than us. My company employs a lot of people. For some of them, it's their primary income. They have families."

My mouth dropped open, his words lost on me. I'm spinning over his regretful tone. With Flynn's resources, I had a chance to save my ass. I have nothing. I'd have to start a new career and the taint of the accusations would follow me around—if I wasn't in jail by then. "You're not going to help me?"

"N-n-no, of course, I will."

If the stutter was resurfacing, I was making him nervous again, but it didn't stop me from pressing. "How? Or should we talk in secret so we aren't seen together?" His expression clouded over and my anger narrowed, spiking like the base of a mushroom cloud. I was an emotional wreck and it clouded my thinking. I'd taken care of myself for so long but suddenly I felt like I couldn't survive without Flynn? I didn't need him. My heart twisted, but I fortified my resolve. I stood up and reached for the leftover chicken breast but snatched my hand back. A small gesture for pride's sake and the beginning of a long, lonely road. "What's your excuse for not helping your sister? I can't imagine her image will take down your empire."

A muscle jumped in Flynn's jaw. His expression was tortured. Worried for me and Lynne—or himself?

I spun and stormed out, my bag flung over my shoulder and knocking into people. I almost shouted, "So sue me!" but this crowd truly would.

Hot tears streamed down my face and I ignored all the faces turned my way. I was so glad I had half a tank of gas I could stretch out for weeks and grateful I hadn't ridden here with Flynn. Why hadn't I learned as a kid? It was me, myself, and I in this world, and in my case, all three of us might go to jail.

CHAPTER 14

illy

Don't cry yet. I listened to the principal explain the terms of my leave. "Yes, sir. No, I understand." I understood he'd drop me like I was Thor's hammer if the school got anything more than a whiff of my turmoil. If this wasn't resolved by the time school started, I might not have a job to go back to. And he'd made it clear that if I got arrested for something like child abuse, I'd be terminated.

I'd never said *fuck my life* after all I'd survived, but it was coming close.

I cruised through the help-wanted ads online. Anything with kids was obviously out. It was like flushing four years of college down the drain.

After the confrontation with Mr. Woods and witnessing the real Flynn Halstengard Tuesday night, I'd come back and cried myself to sleep. Then I'd strapped on my lady balls and searched for work all day yesterday.

Today, I was still unemployed. All my clients had abandoned me, and I wanted to hate them all but couldn't. They had done what they felt was right for their kids, even though I was perfect for their kids, had helped them in so many ways. School was starting in over a month. Would the kids get set up with more tutoring before then? Or would their skills stagnate until then?

Worry gnawed at me. I'd invested so much of myself in their futures, and they were gone. I was off-limits, couldn't even get updates of their progress. If I waited for things to blow over, could I build my business back up, or would rumors circulate and forever tarnish my reputation?

I had a feeling I knew the answer.

My parents. That asshole had tracked down my parents. My dad had blamed me for the dead cat when I'd sobbed over the limp body as my own took the most severe beating of my life.

A car accident? Anyone naïve enough to believe I could break only my jaw in a car accident didn't deserve a dime, much less a fucking bank.

I wanted to lean on Flynn so badly. My platinum-haired knight in shining gym wear, coming to chase away the mean girls throwing litter. Why had he helped me all those years ago? A teen that risked ridicule to do that wouldn't leave his sister.

It was before he'd left home. Before he'd left his mom and Lynne. Was his mom as bad as he'd said? Or was it like my parents, spreading a different story of hate than what had really happened?

I tapped Flynn's name into my computer. I shouldn't waste my time. It wasn't like I had a bunch of calls and messages from him to ignore. But here I was, searching him online. I sifted through several recent articles about him and his work until I found his dad's obituary. A plain and simple article that listed his kids Flynn and Lynne as survivors. The cause of death was drowning.

From the year, Flynn would've been fourteen, maybe fifteen. Poor kid, losing his dad so young and taking care of his mom and sister.

No. I couldn't feel sorry for him when I didn't know his circumstances. He certainly hadn't told me. Nor had he disputed Mr. Woods's insinuation that he was paying his mother off to leave him alone and keep quiet about his sister.

I wanted to believe the best. So badly. Yet he wasn't here. He hadn't called. He'd let me leave and hadn't come after me with an explanation. Despite what Mr. Woods had said about Flynn's mom, his reputation at work meant more.

After all, he hadn't invited me to bring lunch again. As if that moment in the office had exposed us too much. As if he'd never put me on his arm and call me his girlfriend.

There was nothing I could do about him. I had to help myself. Tapping around on my keyboard, I eventually spit out Mrs. Woods's full name. A search turned up nothing. No honors. No top of her class. She'd probably been a spoiled girl who'd gotten her way, then found a man to give her everything she asked for with minimal work.

That hadn't been my future. I'd had to scrounge to keep out of the gutter, and I hadn't stepped on one person to do it. Yet people suspected me of hitting a child when Mrs. Woods was the one with a Hulk-sized cruel streak.

I pulled up Mrs. Blumenthal's number and dialed it. When the woman answered, I explained my dire situation with work and a future income.

"Oh, dear, that's bad. How could they think that of you? But thanks to your man friend, I'll give you two free months of rent. That's what it would've cost if I'd had to pay the deductible."

I slumped, letting my eyelids fall closed. Finding a place

to rent in the cities was hard enough, but a nice and reasonable place was almost impossible. And I had no extra money for a deposit or first and last months' rent. "Thank you so much. I wasn't sure what I'd do. I just need to find a temporary job to tide me over."

"I'll call my son. He's always looking for help in his grocery store in Bloomington. What hours can you work?"

"Anything and everything." For the first time in days, I smiled. Just being able to bring in an income, even save some money, would take a load of stress off my mind.

"Okay, let me call him. Can I give him your number?"

"Of course. And thank you, thank you, thank you."

"It's no problem, Tilly. You're my best tenant, and I don't believe that load of shit for one second."

"Between you and me, I think Charlie's mom beat him." I snapped my mouth shut. Where had that come from? But it made sense. Mrs. Woods was the only other person with consistent access to Charlie. For all Mr. Woods' many, many faults, and no matter how he'd treated me, he seemed to truly care about Charlie's welfare. "I honestly wouldn't put it past her to do it when I was working, or when the nanny was there, so she had someone to blame it on."

"That shouldn't be between you and me, Tilly. Tell the police." After a few more encouragements to hang in there, she hung up.

Who'd believe me, with the pull Mr. Woods had?

Mrs. Blumenthal had my back, though. I sighed. My boyfriend was too concerned about his image to stay by my side, but my landlady believed me. So there was that.

I didn't want to get too excited after the call, so I cruised more help-wanted ads. Scribbling down my choices from best to worst, I listed all the jobs I thought I'd be competent at and where my potential legal woes wouldn't be a problem.

Basically, a place that wouldn't vilify me if word reached them about what I'd been accused of.

My phone rang. For a moment, I fervently hoped it was Flynn checking on me. I didn't recognize the number.

Foolish girl.

I answered. It was Mrs. Blumenthal's son, offering me a job. I could start tomorrow, stocking shelves on the grave-yard shift.

I clicked my phone off after agreeing to start at eleven p.m. the next night. I'd work all weekend, eleven to seven. It wasn't like I had lessons to plan all day for the rest of the summer.

There was a knock at the door. My heart leaped into my throat. Flynn?

I sprinted across the room to answer it. Without even checking the peephole, I swung the door open.

Two police officers, a male, and a female waited on my stoop.

"Tilly Johnson?"

∼

Flynn

"FLYNN? DUDE? MR. HALSTENGARD, SIR?"

I glanced up at the sarcastic tone. Matthew stared at me, one manicured brow raised.

"You never call me Mr. Halstengard."

"Because it'd be a waste of air after two years as your PA. But, dude, you so weren't listening to me. Do you want your hair appointment after your suit fitting so you don't shed little stubs all over new threads you haven't bought yet?"

"Yeah, I don't care." Not one bit. Usually, I did, was very

particular about what I wore and when I upgraded my work clothes. Always the best image possible.

"Seriously." Matthew set his tablet down. "I'm going to step out of bounds here, so fair warning. Now I'm not oblivious. You came back from your bachelor vacation a moody beast. Then you were skiing on rainbows for the last few weeks. I even got home at a decent hour every single night. And you didn't call or leave messages at all on the weekends. Don't think I haven't been dying to know who the cutie is that Mrs. Silverstein was horrified she almost kicked out. What's her name?"

I stared at the door. How many times since that awful night had I wished Mrs. Silverstein would notify me of a girl who'd brought me lunch and wouldn't leave?

Tilly had taken the news of Lynne pretty hard. She'd seemed more hurt that I hadn't been completely honest with her. But the look of total betrayal when she thought I'd chosen my career over her was a knife in the gut every time the image ran through my head. I hadn't seen it that way at the time; I would've been there for her, but every time I came to work and didn't phone my legal department, I imagined myself stomping the knife in her back even deeper.

I hadn't heard more from John. Perhaps I could finish the project and sign off on everything without incident. The man must not have found anything on Tilly. Of course, how would I know?

Matthew snapped his fingers. "You're spacing on me again. Woman's problems?"

"You're right. You're stepping out of bounds."

Matthew's lips pressed together, and he snatched up his tablet like *well then*.

I should apologize. My phone rang. Wes. Was he calling for a golf date? Cuz I could get lost in eighteen holes for a while. It'd take days of eighteen holes to think through the mess I'd made of my life.

"Just a minute," I told Matthew, then answered.

"What. The hell. Is going on?" Wes's voice shook. He was livid.

"What are you talking about? Wait." I sat forward. "Is Tilly okay? Did that bastard get to her?"

"No, Tilly's not okay, fuckwad. Mara just bailed her out. Where the hell were *you*?"

I slammed my hand on the table. Matthew jumped but stayed where he was. "Where is she?"

"Not Arkham anymore, no thanks to you. Mara and I barely got the story out of her in the first place. Then she was incoherent when Mara and I didn't know you two were seeing each other. Why the hell would you keep that secret?"

I sank my face into my free hand. "We haven't talked much in the last few weeks. I've been busy."

"Yeah, with Tilly, I hear. How is all this shit connected?"

"Where is she?" The only thing pushing to the front of my mind was Tilly's well-being. She'd been arrested and thrown in jail. For how long?

Wes let out a breath of frustration. "She's home. She only called because she was frantic to make the first shift of her new job since that asshole blasted her career."

My Tilly wasn't going to sit at home and lose hope. "When does she leave for work?"

It was four o'clock on a Friday. Where would she be working?

"Not till tonight. I guess it's some night-shift job stocking shelves."

I shot up. Matthew's eyes widened. He'd been riveted to my side of the conversation. Tilly was going to be working herself into the ground all night long?

Meanwhile, who the fuck beat that kid and was getting away with it?

"Wes, you helped out Mara with some legal issues, right?"

"No? Oh, you mean the sleazy professor. I would've done that whether she wanted me to or not."

I caught Matthew's gaze. "Your partner's still a cop, right?"

"Yup."

"Does he know legal shit?"

Matthew rolled his eyes. "Please, half his job is pleasing or pissing off lawyers."

"What about cases of child abuse? Does he deal with that?"

He sobered. "More than anyone would realize."

I hit the speaker on the phone. "Okay, guys. I need some help."

illy

I SLOGGED INTO MY PLACE. The hot July sun was already up, and it wasn't even eight in the morning.

My muscles ached. My job—my former job—had been active, but it was nothing like my new one. It was moving my body for eight hours up and down stools, filling bins, lining goods on shelves, emptying boxes.

I'd missed the entire weekend. Work, sleep, repeat was all I'd done.

Because now I had to pay Mara back the bail money. But I now had a court-appointed lawyer. So there was that.

I trudged to my computer. No messages. Nothing on my calendar. I didn't have another shift until the weekend. That meant when I woke up, I'd have to find another job.

Speaking of work. I pulled up the email from my boss at the school. I had resigned, effective immediately. There was no use putting him in the difficult position of prolonging the inevitable. Clearing my name against Mr. Woods's accusations might prove impossible.

Kicking off my shoes, I didn't bother with my clothing. I collapsed into bed and threw an arm over my face. The inability of my blinds to keep out the sun had escaped my notice before now. They were threadbare, and light shone right onto the bed.

My phone rang.

Dammit. Who the hell would bother me at this ungodly hour?

I didn't recognize the number but that wasn't unusual during the past week.

"Tilly Johnson?" It was a woman's voice, someone I didn't know.

"Yep." I kept my arm over my face.

"I'm Luna O'Donnell, the attorney who's been hired for your case."

"Oh, the court-appointed one?" But the guy who'd been at my arraignment had been, well, a guy. And clearly unimpressed with my suspicions in Charlie's case.

"No, ma'am. Flynn Halstengard hired me." I bolted upright and almost dropped the phone. Luna kept talking. "I have some documents to go over with you, and then some questions about your experience with Charles Woods and his dad, John Woods. What time can you meet?"

"Flynn hired you?"

"Yes, ma'am."

"What about his precious business?" Bitterness seeped through my tone, but I was beyond caring.

"The corporation has attorneys assigned to it in that regard. I'm dedicated solely to you."

I couldn't respond. He'd hired me a lawyer. After he'd taken care of his own company. I wasn't nothing to him, but I wasn't his priority, either.

His best friend hadn't even known about us. Flynn was so considerate in private—except for that one time at the theater with Becky. He hadn't proclaimed his love for me, but he hadn't pointed out that I was the crazy lady who'd bid for him, either. So, he'd stood up for me, but at the same time, he hadn't.

Kind of like high school.

He'd been nice enough to me, but he hadn't tried to be my friend or get to know me, Tulip Johnson. Crazy J.

"Miss Johnson, we'd like to conduct our own investigation into the identity of Charlie Woods's abuser. Can we meet to talk?"

Not when I'd been up all night. "Want to find out Charlie's abuser? Let's see, since they couldn't keep a nanny, I'd ask the Stepford mom exactly how Charlie got his bruises."

Luna was quiet on the other end. Was she taking notes, or did she have the blank look my court-appointed attorney had given me?

There was a knock at the door.

"For the love of God, can't a girl get some rest around here?"

"Excuse me, Miss Johnson?"

"Not you. Look, I'm tired and I have to talk to Mr. Halstengard about this arrangement first. But unless you're going to be the kind of lawyer who cares that I don't end up in jail, who'll gun for the real abuser, and who'll legal-speak my parents into the ground for what they said about me, I may as well stick with my listless court-appointed attorney. Thanks." I tossed the phone on the nightstand and went to answer the door Luna already forgotten. Why get her hopes up?

I didn't bother to check who it was. Last time had turned out pretty swell, it's not like it could be worse. I was a hardened criminal now, could take whatever was on the other side of that door.

A rumpled-looking Flynn greeted me. His gaze drank me in like a man starved of water, but I steeled myself. I needed my fortitude to fight the good fight, and from what I'd learned the last time we were together, the good fight wasn't Flynn.

"I, uh… Did a lawyer get ahold of you?"

I draped one hand on the doorknob and the other on my hip. "You'll have to be more specific, Flynn. I suddenly have a lot of lawyers in my life."

"Her name is—"

"Luna something or other. Yes. I don't want your charity." But, dammit, I needed it.

"She's yours. Let her defend you. I get what I did was—"

"What'd you do, Flynn?" I wiggled my fingers by my ears. "Lemme hear it. Because," I barked out a laugh, "it's not like anyone else has. Did you know Wes and Mara knew nothing about us? It's almost August, Flynn. What's that make it? Like, two months since we first had sex?"

"I told you that I'm a private man."

"You weren't supposed to be private with me. I told you my story at the cabin and you neglected to clarify that your sister didn't die. That you're paying off your mom—"

"I'm not bribing her to stay quiet."

I wanted to hear the whole story, but I had enough drama in my life. "It's not my business. I'd just urge you to develop a relationship with your sister. For her sake and yours, but not for mine."

He nodded, a muscle jumping in his jaw. "Tilly, I'm sorry."

"Yeah, I'm sure you are." I could hardly look at him or I'd soften. Had he slept any the whole weekend? "Look, I'll work out a payment plan to reimburse you for Luna's legal fees. I have to pay Mara back first."

"You don't owe me anything. You deserve an apology."

"And you already gave it. Thank you." I yawned and it wasn't for effect. "I've been up all night and I'm very tired. Thanks again, Flynn."

"Tilly, d-d-don't block me out. We can get through this, together. I-I love you."

I stilled and met his earnest emerald gaze. Why was the admission hard for him to say? Did he even know what love should be like? I could crumble and throw myself into his arms, and I had a strong impulse to do just that. But while he might love me, he still wasn't offering things my upbringing had taught me to treasure, like respect, trust, and honesty. The drive to move heaven and earth to take care of the one you loved.

Flynn might love me, but he lacked the rest.

"And I love you, too, Flynn. But you know what? It's not enough. My parents loved me, too. I truly think they did. No, you're nothing like them, but in a way, you are. I want your acceptance. I want your respect. I want you to make an effort at a real relationship. You love me. I believe you love your sister. But until you learn how to be in a relationship of any kind, I can't do this." I swiped at a tear rolling down my cheek. Flynn's expression grew bleak. "I fought for my childhood and now I have to fight for my adulthood and I won't settle for pretty words. I...I want to know I'm safe with you."

"I got the lawyer..."

She leveled her gaze on him, let him see how serious she was. "Did you do that after I was arrested?" His silence was my answer. "Do you know what that tells me? That you waited to see if it'd all blow over and you could save your precious account. So your lawyer is too little too late. And I understand if you pull her help because it's not winning me back. But I'm done being your little secret."

Stepping back to shut the door, I risked one last glance.

His hair stuck up in all directions, shadows hung under his eyes, and his shoulders drooped. He was far removed from the brawny roofer of a few weeks ago. "Tilly. I'll do anything."

I swallowed hard. "You had your chance. You had so many chances," I said raggedly.

The door clicked shut. I hung my head.

That should've been the hardest thing I had to do, but it wasn't even close.

illy

THREE MONTHS LATER...

I wrung my hands together. Was it too obvious? My old boss couldn't give me my original job back, but I was in his office begging for anything else he had available.

A yawn snuck up on me. I tried stifling it but had to cover my mouth. Months on the night shift and it was still brutal on my system. Add in weekdays full of cleaning rooms at a hotel and it equaled no days off.

Mr. Person watched me carefully. "The charges were dropped, you say?"

"Yes." How'd I explain it and leave my personal life personal? "Um, the company the accuser was blackmailing," my heart wrenched just thinking of Flynn, wondering what he was doing now, "took on the case, and after a thorough investigation, they discovered that Charlie's mom, the child's mom, was abusing him."

It was over. My lawyer had even heeded my wishes and discussed the legal ramifications about lying to law enforcement with my parents. They'd retracted their claims and promised to never think about me again.

Yay, me. If it weren't for Mrs. B, I would be absolutely and completely alone in the world.

Mr. Person pushed up his glasses, his features grim. "How is Charlie doing?"

"Good, actually. His dad's a piece of work, pardon my opinion, but at least he's fighting for his son."

"What company was he blackmailing? Excuse the questions, but what you went through doesn't happen every day, thank goodness."

"Halstengard Industries." It hurt to say it. I wrung my hands. "They parted ways, I guess." Flynn's lawyers had been excellent. The best money could buy, and unlike Mr. Woods's county attorney, honest. And when Mr. Woods found out his wife was behind Charlie's injuries, he'd diverted his attention to his divorce and trying to keep his wife from getting half their assets.

"Have you picked up any tutoring?"

I smiled sadly. "No. I've notified my former clients, but none of them have taken me back." They'd moved on to another tutor, or the seed of doubt had been planted and they couldn't bring themselves to trust me again. I couldn't dwell on it. If I ruminated about all I'd lost in the last few months, I'd wither away in depression.

"Sorry to hear. You excel at working with the kids." He spread his hands and my hopes sank. I knew what was coming next. "I'm sorry. We filled your position and we have a full house. Not even a paraprofessional slot open. I'll certainly keep you in mind, and don't hesitate to use me as a reference."

I hid my dismay behind a smile and thanked him for his

time. All of this could've been done over the phone, but I knew he'd wanted to meet with me and gauge how I'd changed, see if I was someone he'd offer a job to again.

I wandered out of the school where I used to spend my days. None of my kids were in the halls and I hadn't the heart to request a visitor's pass. Seeing them with their new teacher would be more bitter than sweet. I could only be so optimistic.

But I still had my teaching license and a clear record. That was a start.

This was my first full day off that didn't include legal meetings. Whatever should I do?

Stop at Arcadia? Now that I had some change in my pockets, I could buy myself a pick-me-up. Mara had been paid back and Luna had said that if I tried to reimburse the law firm, it'd be a financial headache and to please let them keep it pro bono.

Only it hadn't been. Flynn had footed the bill.

How was he doing?

Argh. I only asked myself that fifty times a day—on a slow day.

I'd meant it. I loved him. But after my childhood, security came first.

Had he gone back to old habits and women like Becky?

No, no shopping today. Mara called and checked on me constantly, but I needed that distance. The difficulty in not asking about Flynn grew harder each time.

For the end of October, the weather was lovely. I wore an old cardigan and slip-ons that I often didn't get to wear when teaching because they were too boring. A walk, perhaps? I'd go home and change shoes and enjoy the weather before the wind turned so cold it hurt my face to be outside.

A refreshing walk sounded better and better as I drove home. I jogged inside and tossed off my sandals. In my room,

I found socks in the basket of clean laundry I had no time to fold because I was always working. Stuffing my feet into my shoes I breezed outside and—

Ran into a solid chest.

"Whoa. Is there something wrong?"

That voice vibrated through my body straight down to my toes. I gasped and looked up. Flynn's hands were on my shoulders.

Flynn's hands were on my shoulders?

I jerked out of his reach and stumbled over the doorstep. He caught me again.

"Sorry," I said and righted myself far out of his reach.

He seemed reluctant to let me go, or perhaps that was my wishful thinking.

An old shard of fear stuck in my throat. Was it not really over? Had it been a dream that I'd gotten some semblance of my life back? "What are you doing here?"

"I came to pick you up. I need to show you something."

I stared at him. He came to pick me up when I happened to have a day off, the first in months? "Mara told you I was home."

He nodded.

God, he looked good, but where was the suit? It was the middle of the week. He was wearing jeans and a cable-knit sweater that folded over at the neck. Very stylish, very casual. Very unlike Flynn.

"Aren't you working today?" I asked.

"Yes, that's why I'm here. Come on." He turned and walked to his truck like he expected me to just follow. More like he knew the curiosity would get to me and I'd do what he asked.

The pang of seeing his truck sitting at my curb again was too much. He opened the passenger door and cocked his head toward it. Movement inside caught my attention. There was someone else in there.

The curiosity angle worked. My legs started moving.

"I hope you don't mind if we have company." He'd lost the light tone.

I reached the door and peered in. "Oh. Hi."

A woman was in the back. She was blond, like Flynn, but her hair was chopped at chin length. One hand curled into her abdomen and she canted to the side as she sat.

"Lynne," Flynn called over my shoulder, "this is Tilly, the girl I told you about."

"I— You—" Tilly shook her head. "Hi, Lynne."

I hadn't expected Flynn to see his sister. Ensure she was in a good home, maybe visit once to ease his guilty conscience, but Lynne was *here*, in his truck.

Lynne made a soft noise and raised her functioning hand a few inches from her lap.

"She says hi," Flynn said.

"Hello." I waved in return and climbed inside. I turned to his sister. "Now you need to tell me why you're out joyriding with your brother."

The door shut behind Tilly. The corner of Lynne's mouth lifted in a smile, her gaze tracking her brother around the truck. She gestured to the driver's side.

"Flynn's idea, huh? I have to admit, my curiosity is killing me."

Flynn hopped in and shot me a grin. He twisted back to give Lynne a wink before he threw the pickup into drive.

What was he up to? This Flynn reminded me of the guy at the lake. The one who'd let down most of his guard and watched movies and even eaten some carbs. This Flynn looked like he only had a six-pack instead of an eight-pack and like he got home at a decent time many nights of the week.

When we got back on the road, I peeked at him, but it was like looking into the sun. I was back in his truck, surrounded by hints of his cologne. Memories jarred me. Laughter, love, sex. He'd taught me how to fish.

"I can't do this, I'm sorry." I even reached for the door handle while we were moving. "You can just drop me off here."

"Tilly, please. This is about more than you and me."

That stopped me. My moment of panic passed, and I drew in a deep breath. "Okay. Why don't you fill me in on what's going on in your life?"

"As you can see, I tracked down Lynne. My lawyer worked with my mom." He spoke under his breath, "Bought her out." He switched back to regular volume. "And I found a private group home for her where they even put her to work. Right, Lynne?"

Lynne murmured her agreement.

Flynn nodded. "She's a greeter at a store close by the home. I've hired an organization that'll take her to work and help her through her shift."

I shifted in my seat so I could see both Lynne and Flynn. "That's awesome, Lynne. You'll have to tell me where and when you work so I can stop by." And I would, no matter what I had to buy.

Flynn's voice dropped. "How've you been, Tilly?"

I stayed where I was. I wasn't sure what Lynne could understand, but I didn't want to exclude her. "I work two jobs and have no life. But I'm not in jail, thanks to you, so things are well."

"Mara said you had an interview for your old teaching position."

"It was more of an 'I'm dying to know what happened' than an interview."

"That sucks."

"Yeah."

We fell quiet. Occasionally Lynne would make a sound that I couldn't decipher, but Flynn would chatter back to her about buildings they were passing, guessing at what she'd been trying to tell him.

He pulled up to a vacant lot on the edge of town. There were a few surrounding businesses, office spaces mostly, and a gas station on the corner.

"Where are we?"

Reaching behind the front seat, he pulled out a roll of paper. "Lynne, do you mind if I hop outside with Tilly and explain everything?"

Lynne lifted her hand like before.

"Thanks, Sis." Flynn hopped out and rushed to my side of the vehicle.

I raised a curious brow at Lynne but the girl had already gone back to staring out the window. The door opened, and Flynn offered his hand to help me out. I fortified myself against the strength and warmth of his grip. He didn't release my hand as he led me around to the front of the pickup. When he let go to spread out the paper, I missed the contact.

I seized the moment of privacy. "May I ask—how was the reunion?"

His gaze flicked to the windshield. Lynne still gazed outside as if fascinated by the scenery. And if she'd been stuck inside for years, she probably was.

"I don't think she knew me. I…" He clenched his jaw and scowled at the hood of the pickup. "It was hard for me. The last time I'd seen her, she'd almost drowned again in the bathtub. I was bathing her and trying to clean her chair at the same time and left her alone too long."

I laid a hand on his arm. "That was when you left home?" He'd only been sixteen. The poor kid. No wonder he'd been so traumatized. His mother had probably laid all the blame at his teenage feet. He'd probably felt that Lynne was better off without him and had justified his absence with his guilt. "She's a survivor and you were a kid."

He nodded, his throat working as if he didn't trust himself to speak.

"But she knows you now. That's obvious."

A smile lit his handsome face, chasing away the shadows of the past. "She loves to go for rides. I steal her every weekend. Her communication's limited, but I'm learning."

"I'm very happy for you."

"The tour of my office scared her, I think, but now she's like a celebrity when she visits."

I gaped at him. He'd gone from not telling anyone about his sister to the red-carpet treatment. My Flynn? "I mean it. I'm happy for you."

He cleared his throat. "So that's us, but we're here for you." He gestured to the empty space. "We are at the future Center for Specialized Development. That's just a preliminary name so we had something to call the project."

"What?" I peered closer at the sheaf of large papers he held. Blueprints. On one sheet was the image of a building with three wings, and between each wing was a small courtyard. "Wait, what?"

"I'm building your tutoring center. And it needs a manager."

I stared at him. At the blueprints. At the vacant lot.

"Or you can hire a manager if you just want to teach. Either way, the place is yours."

"Mine," I squeaked. "How can you give me a *building*?"

"Halstengard Industries will provide the scholarships. You figure out the details."

"How— Why?"

"Because I love you, Tilly. And I'll do anything for you, even stay away for three months while I figure this business out and talk myself into being okay if you turn me down. One thing I learned looking into places where Lynne can live in a well-rounded environment is that there's a serious lack of resources. The community needs a center like this, one that doesn't have to worry so hard about keeping the doors open, one where the clients don't have to sit and wonder how the hell they're going to pay for it. With or without me by your side, the place will be your baby."

"Mine?"

He still loved me. I shook my head. This was too much. Information overload. I went from fighting not to collapse in despair to having my wildest dreams handed to me. I should turn it down, but that'd mean handing over the care of all the future kids to someone else. Giving this up, now that I knew it existed and could be my project, was too much. But accepting it, accepting him, overwhelmed me.

"I'm serious, Tilly. It's yours to run, no strings."

"It needs a different name" was all I could say. It confirmed nothing. I wasn't ready to commit to either him or the center.

"Take all the time you need. I'll be patient. Persistent, but patient. By the way, Wes and Mara have set up a scholarship for families, too."

Wes was *loaded*. A place like this, with the continual support of those two businesses? Unreal. "You're unbelievable."

"I also have a standing contribution set up for the Center for Abuse Recovery. Each year, they'll receive a donation in your name." He ran his finger along the design. "I wasn't sure about the layout. I had a lot of meetings with other therapy places and came up with this."

The man who worked twelve- to fourteen-hour days on his own business? "When'd you have time for all this?"

"Matthew. Two years of following me around, he knows

all the people and all the lingo. Add in Mrs. Silverstein, and they're unstoppable."

"Your PA is running your company?" More importantly, Flynn had handed over the reins to someone else? That it was Matthew made sense, at least. Flynn trusted him.

"He's not a PA anymore. That level mostly needs a salesman and Matthew can smooth talk with the best of them. I still work, too, just not as much."

"So what do you do with all your free time now besides joyride?"

His gaze turned sincere. "Try to build a safe life for you."

"I can't just…" I couldn't finish. Because the thought of just jumping in with him terrified me.

"I know." His large hand wrapped around mine. "And it's okay. I'm here when you're ready."

I stared at where our hands were intertwined. "You're here now."

"Yes. For as long as you'll let me."

I glanced at the vacant lot. The image on the blueprints was hard to envision over the weeds and uneven ground, but Flynn could make it a reality. For me. He'd offered me heaven, love, *and* everything that went with it. And he was going to move earth to make my dreams come true.

"I've been miserable without you." Way to hold on to my resolve. Be strong. Make him earn it. But he was my kryptonite and he was serious. The center, Lynne, waiting until plans were in place before he came to my house—none of that was merely talk. He was sincere, and he was making strides to change his ways.

He dropped a kiss on my forehead, his warm lips lingering on my skin, as good as branding me. It ignited all the cravings that had haunted each night I'd spent alone. "Misery doesn't begin to describe it, Tilly. I thought I had little purpose in life outside of work. Then you left. When I wasn't busy with Lynne or these plans, I was reminiscing about every second we spent together." His voice dropped to a low growl that curled my toes. "Some more than others."

"Ohmigod. Me, too."

We both laughed. I squeezed his hand. He'd been there for me when I thought he'd abandoned me. He'd already waited patiently. We'd known each other for years—enough time had been wasted. "Have you and Lynne eaten yet? I'm starving, and I need to hear all about this crazy, fabulous idea of yours. I think I have a new name for it."

EPILOGUE

*F*lynn

One year later...

"Ready for this?" I grinned at Tilly. My wife's cheeks were flushed with excitement and she hadn't quit smiling all day.

Tilly looked up at the sign that read *Crazy J's Learning Center* and grinned. "Absolutely. But it's hard to hold these scissors." Because they were as tall as she was.

"Let me help. Smile for the cameras." I took the burden of the weight, which I'd been insisting on since we'd arrived. But she'd argued, *How often does one get to hold a five-foot-tall pair of scissors?*

She took a moment to straighten her tiara. This one was flashy and full of fake sparkle. One of my favorites. I liked seeing her in them and now that she was back to being around kids all day, she donned them more often.

I was going to buy her a real one for Christmas.

I posed with her to cut the ribbon. Wes and Mara stood off to the side with Lynne, and Chris the co-owner of Arcadia even found a replacement to come support our cause. He joked about being the third wheel at the store now that I had Tilly and Wes had Mara. *Maybe this store will bring drop a love life in my lap as it did with Mara and Tilly.* I held out hope for him. I was too stinking happy not to, and Chris was on to something. Arcadia brought me and Tilly together just like it did with Wes and Mara.

I glanced back at the little group of my friends and family. Mara cradled her little son. I would never forget when the call came from Wes, the exuberant first-time dad.

"It's a boy. Samuel Clark."

Wes's dad had been named Sam, but I couldn't remember a Clark in his family tree. *"As in Clark Kent? Why not Kal-El?"*

"Fuck you. When you have a kid named Harley or Quinn, I'm going to remember this moment."

I had laughed, but I could envision it happening whether I and Tilly had a boy or a girl. The thought of having kids no longer gave me palpitations. I might be a dad someday. I was basically an uncle now. I'd gone back to being a brother. My mom had said she'd start therapy, but I wasn't holding out hope. Ultimately, I wanted her to get help, but I couldn't have her toxicity around my family until she did.

Lynne had more health troubles than I'd anticipated, but on days like today, she could hang out with us. And I made sure she did regularly. Tilly had named one wing of the center after her.

I took it all in. My new life. The new center that had brought Tilly back to me.

There'd be no clients today, just celebrating. The rest of the week would be staff orientation, then sessions would start. Many parents had called asking for in-home tutoring, but Tilly couldn't bring herself to tackle that just yet. I had made sure the building was wired with cameras so no session went unmonitored. If she started an outreach program, I'd do nothing short of equipping her staff with body cams.

But that venture could wait. Coming off our wedding and a month-long honeymoon at Lake Webber in our cabin, she was diving into running a business, and I was dedicated to making her blissfully happy.

Shortly after I'd pretty much begged her to take me back, she'd quit both of her jobs and moved in with me. Our house had one room just for her Wacky Monday wear. Items my size was now in the collection because I'd been informed that if I wanted to drop by on Mondays, I had to look the part. Anything the missus wanted, she got.

When she was busy at work, and Matthew had all the bases covered at the office, I'd found myself a new hobby. I'd bought the rental house from Mrs. Blumenthal and made it my winter project. Then I'd found another rental house in sore need of updating, and I had my eye on a third. The musty smell of dilapidated places and the memories it elicited no longer bothered me like they used to.

After the ribbon-cutting and pictures, Tilly towed me inside. I pulled her into my side and draped an arm across her shoulders.

She grinned up at me. "I can't believe this is done. That we're already at this point. Are you going to take on another project at work?"

"Nope." I was split in a lot of directions, but I also staffed accordingly now instead of doing nothing but work. My job was no longer an excuse to hide from life. I was surrounded by reasons to get out of the office and loosen my tie—or not wear one at all. "I have the perfect woman and I need to be her Puddin'."

Chris dedicates his life to Arcadia, but when he meets a

mysterious woman at comic con, he learns how off limits she is. First to Fail

I'd love to know what you thought. Please consider leaving a review for First to Bid at the retailer the book was purchased from.

For all the latest news, sneak peeks, quarterly short stories, and free material sign up for my newsletter.

ABOUT THE AUTHOR

Marie Johnston writes paranormal and contemporary romance and has collected several awards in both genres. Before she was a writer, she was a microbiologist. Depending on the situation, she can be oddly unconcerned about germs or weirdly phobic. She's also a licensed medical technician and has worked as a public health microbiologist and as a lab tech in hospital and clinic labs. Marie's been a volunteer EMT, a college instructor, a security guard, a phlebotomist, a hotel clerk, and a coffee pourer in a bingo hall. All fodder for a writer!! She has four kids and even more cats.

mariejohnstonwriter.com

Follow me:

ALSO BY MARIE JOHNSTON

First To Lie

First to Bid

First to Fail

Printed in Great Britain
by Amazon

69943081R00113